MW01267797

PANDORA'S GAME

Other Works by Christopher Andrews

NOVELS

Dream Parlor
Paranormals
Hamlet: Prince of Denmark

COLLECTIONS

The Darkness Within

SCREENPLAYS

Thirst
Dream Parlor
(written with Jonathan Lawrence)
Mistake

THEATRICAL PLAYS

Duet

VIDEO GAMES

Bankjob

PANDORA'S GAME

A Novel by
CHRISTOPHER ANDREWS

Copyright © 1999 by Christopher Andrews

Pandora's Game

ISBN Number: Paperback 0-9774535-2-9

All rights reserved. No part of this book may be reproduced or transmitted in any form or by any means electronic or mechanical, including photocopying, recording, or by any information storage and retrieval system, without permission in writing from the copyright owner.

This is a work of fiction. Names, characters, places, and incidents are either the product of the creator's imagination or are used fictitiously, and any resemblance to any actual persons, living or dead, events, or locales is entirely coincidental.

This book was printed in the United States of America.

First Rising Star Visionary Press edition: February, 2006

**A Rising Star Visionary Press book
for extra copies please contact by e-mail at
risingstarvisionarypress@earthlink.net
or send by regular mail to
Rising Star Visionary Press
Copies Department
P O Box 9226
Fountain Valley, CA 92728-9226**

Thanks to the *Deathtrap* gang,
Kenton Bishop, Mike Desper,
and Joel Carpenter.

Also to Mark Brotherton, Nora Burns,
David Vance, Camden Campbell,
Jamie & Tawnya Baxter,
Anita Barrett, Akie Blounts,
Jonathan Lawrence, Shizuka Takayasu,
and, of course, Mom & Dad.

And this Rising Star edition
is especially dedicated to
Yvonne Kristina Isaak-Andrews,
my wife, editor, and Imzadi.

FOREWORD
by Delano Carpenter

The story you are about to read was written by my son, Neil. It's all I have left of him, and I feel obligated to make it known. I don't know how it will be received. To be honest, with all the madness happening in the world right now, I'm not sure how to take it myself.

I hope you'll forgive me if I sound a bit disjointed. Writing is not my area of expertise. That's one of Neil's many fortes. Unfortunately, my wife hasn't been dealing with recent events very well, so the responsibility has fallen to me. I'll give you what little background I know.

First, there are some facts here that I can personally confirm. Neil's life behind the scenes, of course; the fact that he majored in theatre at college, and that he took a Psychology class and staged *Deathtrap* last semester. More specific to the story, you can ask anyone about the recent murders that have the whole state in an uproar.

Over the few months that this story covers, I didn't spend as much time with my son as I would have liked. That isn't just the regretful musing of a parent looking back. His theatre degree and other activities (which I now know included hypnosis) left him with little free time. I was proud of him, yes, but still missed seeing him.

When I did see him, he never seemed to be under any unusual duress. Granted, he was an actor, but he was also my son. If he was growing ... *unbalanced*, he hid it well.

Five days ago, Neil came to me and asked if he could spend some time in our trailer home up by Lake Thunderbird. When I asked him why, he merely told me he had "some things he wanted to get down on paper," and that he thought the seclusion would help him write faster. Well, Neil was an actor *and* a writer, and writers are sometimes *eccentric*, so I gave him the keys. I actually suspected he might be taking a girlfriend with him, although I have since learned that this was not the case.

Two days ago, the police rang my doorbell. It seemed they wanted to ask Neil a few questions concerning these recent, bizarre murders. I'd seen the news, and my stomach churned at the thought of Neil's being involved, but I quickly agreed to escort them to our lot at the lake. If Neil *were* involved, I thought we could help him better by cooperating right from the start.

When I unlocked the door to the trailer, I felt my heart in my throat. His car was parked outside, but inside we found nothing. Neil was gone. He hasn't been seen or heard from by anyone since I sent him on his way last week.

Yesterday morning, I found this manuscript in an envelope in my mailbox. It had been placed there sometime in the night and addressed to "Mom and Dad," although I don't recognize the handwriting.

That's everything I knew, leading up to the reading of this story. Is it true? It can't be, of course. But it was written by my son, and he apparently believed every word of it. So here it is. Make of it what you will. Neil, if you're out there and see these words, please come home. Your mother and I are worried sick, and we will do everything we can to help you.

And if *you* really are reading these words, Mr. Bachman, then *damn you* for what you've done to my son!

Delano Carpenter

GENESIS

ONE

Russian Roulette.

A standard, six-chamber revolver. One bullet.

Load the gun, spin the chamber, press the barrel to your head, squeeze the trigger.

Simple rules, simpler results. Five-in-six wins you a chance to brag about your immense bravery. The alternative needs no explanation.

A lot of people associate this game with the movie *The Deer Hunter*. A multitude of similar wagers with basic rule variations exist, but they all boil down to the same thing: A gamble with your life.

Russian Roulette is the extreme example with which most people cannot truly identify. After all, what idiot in his right mind would willingly aim a loaded gun at himself, right?

Unfortunately, not all games of deadly chance are so conspicuous, so clearly foolish or demented. We don't always see them for what they are. Sometimes, with ignorance paving our way, we play games with fire.

And we get *burned*.

Tonight is a dark and stormy night. Sounds cliche, but it happens to be true. As I sit here and scrawl in longhand the only written account of my incredible experiences, I can hear the rain spattering against the roof of this trailer, the constant creaking of the torrential wind against the thin walls, and the frequent thunder rolling through the clouds above. I see the lightning flashes from the corner of my eye, and occasionally the lamp light flickers and threatens to fade altogether. I couldn't ask for a more appropriate night to record these memoirs. The only thing missing is a voice-over by Vincent Price.

My name is Neil Carpenter. Neil Joshua Carpenter. But if you were to catch me off guard, perhaps if I were sleepy or distracted, and you asked me what my name is, I might very well turn to you, look you straight in the eye, and answer, "Alistaire Bachman."

Right now, at this moment, I can remember most of what has happened to me over the last few months. At any given point, I may actually be recounting something here on this paper that I *didn't* have any real knowledge of at the time. But, for the present, Alistaire Bachman is graciously allowing me full access to my own mind, and I don't want to waste the opportunity.

My life prior to ... *encountering* Alistaire Bachman was somewhat short of note. I had my share of friends, played trumpet for seven years, oil painted every now and then, got hooked on acting in the eighth grade, collected comic books, and enjoyed creative writing. I'm the older of two brothers, lost my first grandparent last year, and have had a few girlfriends.

The events that led up to my recent troubles started early last semester. I was a Junior at the University of Oklahoma, diligently working on my Theatre degree, and I'd been hanging out with a guy named Mark Hudson.

Mark and I had been bumping into one another for years at the theatre department without ever really getting to know each other. Then we both got stuck costume-crewing the same show, and we hit it off great. It turned out we had a lot of the same interests, read the same kinds of books, watched the same kinds of movies. Pretty soon we were spending a lot of time together. Mark sort of fell into acting after starting out as an Art major. He'd spend hours doodling in his notebook, sketching caricatures of people around the department and posting them on the call board. I'd seen his art countless times and admired it for what it was, but it wasn't until I got a glimpse of his real, hardcore art that I realized his true talent.

It was a Sunday night. Mark was over at my place for our usual weekend ritual of watching "Star Trek." Afterward we always talked for a while about this and that, how the school productions were going, which professors issued too much homework ... nothing special, just shootin' the shit, so to speak. Mark was wanting a new book to read, so I suggested he go through the pile at the foot of my bed.

Between my copies of *Refuge Among the Stars* and *Dream Parlor*, Mark found an issue of my homemade comic book series. In the second grade, my teacher had us take three sheets of regular notebook paper, fold them in half, and make our own comic books as a lesson in creativity. The idea stuck with me, and to that day I made little comics as a hobby.

"What's this?" he asked, flipping open my seventeenth issue of "The Invincible Team."

"Mmm? Oh. Nothing really." I explained my hobby to him. He sat on the edge of the bed and quickly read the short comic. It kind of embarrassed me to let him read it; I'm a much better *writer* than *artist*.

He closed the little book and retrieved his note pad. "I want to show you something," he said. Finding the appropriate pages, he turned it over and handed it to me.

I raised an eyebrow at what I saw. It was an impressive — *very* impressive — sketch of a woman in leather sporting a sword in one hand and a gun in another. She was crouched as if to spring, the tension in her muscles well captured. Her long, dark hair swirled in a way that suggested her head had just whipped around into this pose. The art was as good as any I'd seen in Marvel, DC, or any other professional comics.

"Check out the next few pages," he suggested, sounding both timid and excited.

Every page displayed a single figure, usually armed to the teeth and drawn in pencil. A tall, black man in rags leaning against a dead tree. An elf-like woman landing from an apparent somersault. A hideously deformed man leveling his one-armed cannon at the viewer. The drawings were far better than anything I'd seen him do around the department, caricature or otherwise.

"What are these from?" I asked.

"I made them up. What do you think?" he asked as I handed back the note pad. That same apprehension and eagerness in his voice suggested not many people had seen them.

"They're good," I told him honestly. "I'm serious. They are *really* good. You ought to submit them to Marvel or somebody."

"I've thought about it," he admitted, "but I'm not sure I could handle a letter telling me I have no talent."

I laughed. "Honestly, Mark, I *really* don't think you have to worry about that. They're *excellent*. I mean it."

"Thanks," he said. "You'll have to let me read more of your comics sometime."

I scrunched my face into a tight ball of disgust. "After seeing how good *you* are, I'd rather not."

Blushing, he grinned and glanced at his watch. "I'd better get going. 'Play Structure and Analysis' is going to come way too early." Mark gathered his things and I saw him to the door. As he headed for the stairs, he glanced back and chuckled, "You know, we ought to do a comic *together* sometime. You write it, I draw it." He waved. "Later!"

Mark's suggestion didn't really soak in until after I'd gone to bed. Doing a comic together ... I had always wanted a shot at doing comics, but it's hard to break into the big companies without knowing someone, and I certainly couldn't draw well enough to do my own and submit them to an independent. The longer I thought about Mark's illustrations, the more impressed I was.

My head began spinning with ideas. What kind of stories could we do? We couldn't do "The Invincible Team." I'd started that series when I was in the fifth grade, and the characters would be way too corny without a major overhaul. Besides, Mark's drawings had been very gothic, very dark. If that was his forte, I thought I should try to stick to that.

My thoughts turned to other stories I'd written. Which ones might work as a comic series? *The Blue Man*? No, it was a ghost story, but it was self-contained, not episodic enough to warrant an ongoing saga. *The Marshland*? Nah. *Heart of Steel*? Not dark enough to fit Mark's style.

Then it hit me. Not so much a former story as a *concept*, one I'd never even titled. I'd read an occasional story about a vampire who wasn't all that bad, or a werewolf who controlled his animal fury. What if a small group of such supernatural beings banded together for the common good? I'd decided on a trio — a vampire, a werewolf, and a zombie — but nothing else had come from the idea until now.

The more I thought about it, the more episodic it seemed. A vampire who never drank human blood ... no, let's say that he never took it *directly* from the living, never took a victim. A werewolf with phenomenal control over his lycanthropy, except during the full moon, at which time he voluntarily locked himself up. And a zombie ... well, George A. Romero depicted them as cannibals in *Night of the Living Dead*. So, a zombie who never ate human flesh.

Yeah. I had something here.

I couldn't sleep now. My excitement built until I finally decided to call Mark.

He'd just gotten into bed himself when he answered. "What's up?"

"Mark, how serious were you when you suggested that we do a comic together?"

He paused a beat. "I don't know ... pretty serious, I guess. Why, you interested?"

"I think so. Wanna hear my idea?"

"Shoot."

His enthusiasm built as I described the concept to him.

"I like that," he said. "I like that a *lot*."

"Good. Tell you what. Meet me in the Green Room tomorrow after Acting class. Bring your notepad and we'll kick around a few ideas ..."

We talked for a while longer, pitching back and forth mundane issues like the characters' genders, countries of origin, stuff like that, until we finally realized that we *had* to try to get some sleep.

Sounds harmless enough, doesn't it? Simple, meaningless. Just two friends talkin', two guys with an idea.

How could I have known?

*   *   *

The Green Room was filled with its usual clouds of cigarette smoke and clusters of theatre and dance students. People sat around on well-worn, ugly couches and chairs, talking about everything from test results to the latest dating gossip. Two Coke machines, a snack machine, and a coffee, tea, and juice machine lined two walls, and there were more trash cans and ash trays than you could shake a stick at. Mark was sitting on an especially battered brown couch in one of the corners.

"I'll have you know," Mark told me as I sat next to him, "that I didn't get any sleep last night, thanks to you."

"Really?" I slipped my backpack from my shoulder and onto the floor next to me. "Any progress?"

"Much. You?"

"Some. I've come up with the names for each character, rough backgrounds, that sort of thing. Still haven't thought of a title though."

"How about this?" He handed me his notepad and lit up a cigarette.

Across the top of the page, in large, creepy-style letters, stood the word, *"TRIUMVIRATE."*

"Cool." I offered the pad back.

"Hoped you'd like it. Keep flipping."

The first sketch was a broad-chested, wide-shouldered black man of very impressive size. He wore rugged jeans with no shoes and a white T-shirt with a picture of Mickey Mouse on the front. In his left hand he held a large Lego piece. His expression was totally void of emotion, and his eyes were deliberately blank, the irises without pupils. The man sat cross-legged, his vacant gaze regarding the plastic toy.

"The zombie," Mark told me. "If we're going with the 'Living Dead' slant, then I figure he'd be pretty slow on the uptake. Maybe even *childlike*, peaceful until provoked."

"We think alike," I said. "I picture him spending half his time watching 'Sesame Street.' " With his permission, I jotted the name *"TREY MATTHEWS"* at the bottom of the page.

I flipped to the next page. Another casually dressed man, this time Caucasian. His build was also taut and defined, though not nearly as overbearing as the zombie's. A thick mane of hair swept back over his head to hang just above the collar of his black T-shirt, and bushy sideburns ran down each cheek about three inches. A faint smile danced on his lips and his eyes issued a friendly, personable sparkle. I gave Mark a little thumbs-up, scribbled *"SEAN MALLORY"* below it, and turned the page once more.

There he stood. An immaculate, expensive gray suit, crafted from the finest silk. A tall, slender and yet powerful frame. Strong, fine hands, the nail on each finger a little long but otherwise a manicurist's vision. Chiseled features, potent jaw, dark, wavy hair that fell perfectly into place. Only the whites of his eyes peaked from behind squinted lids, even as pronounced canines lurked between slightly parted lips.

"Hello, Alistaire Bachman."

II

The older man pushed the cup across the counter. He smiled kindly and suggested, "You might wanna drink it here, son. This ain't the safest part of town to be walkin' around, not at this hour. 'Specially for a tourist. Why concha stick around for a while?"

The Irishman took the hot coffee and returned the smile. Little did the considerate old fellow know that he was a far cry more deadly than most muggers could ever dream. Still, this was his first trip to America, and the Big Apple, and he was in just as much danger of getting lost as the next man. So he paid for his drink and agreed, "Sure, why not? Do ye mind if I take a look at the menu while I'm at it?"

"'Course! Gotta make a livin', might as well take advantage of my captive audience, right?" The man laughed heartily at his own joke and gave Sean a greasy, laminated sheet. Sean chuckled out of courtesy and headed for a booth. He took a load off of his tired feet and stretched, then took a long sip. He'd have preferred a beer, but this humble establishment unfortunately did not come equipped with a liquor license.

Oh, well. He'd live.

So, this was America. New York, New York. Sean had heard about it, read about it, and seen it in the movies and on the telly, but to actually be here and experiencing it was an entirely different thing. In the hours since he'd gotten off the plane, it seemed as though his heightened olfactory had picked up more scents than he'd ever experienced in all of his homeland put together. Even Dubland was dwarfed by the sheer immensity *of the place. Impressive, to say the least.*

Sean settled in and looked over the menu. Not much of what he saw appealed to him — the steak, assuming he could get it rare, was the only thing even in the neighborhood — but now he felt obligated to order something, *so he opened his mouth to call the old guy over.*

The door opened, reminding Sean that in the reputed City That Never Sleeps, two middle-of-the-night guests would be nothing out of the ordinary. But when the newcomer stepped inside, Sean realized almost instantly that "ordinary" was the last *quality he could apply to this man.*

He wore a fine suit that must have been Armani, or some other design that required a credit check just to touch it. He floated into the diner with a gliding step that suggested both grace and power. What, exactly, was he *doing in a place like* this?

Sniff. *No doubt about it, this guy was* not *human. Sean didn't detect any trace of werewolf redolence, either, so that left one big possibility ... and it* didn't *make him a very happy Irishman.*

Great, *he thought.* My first night in the States, and I run into one of the local undead.

The vampire — assuming that's what he was, and Sean for one had few doubts — moved fluidly toward the counter and the old cook, then he stopped. He turned his head, and locked eyes with Sean. A heartbeat passed, and the creature was headed Sean's way.

Here we go.

Sean tensed. He tried to avoid the damned beasts whenever he could, but if this one was looking for trouble, then he'd find Sean Mallory up to the challenge. Sean started to rise, to draw the fight outside and away from the cook if he could ...

... and something inside told him to hold off a moment. As the vampire drew closer, Sean watched for changes, any indication that the man was preparing to ... well, to vamp out *on him. But there was nothing. The man was keeping his supernatural characteristics in low gear, and* that *did not fit someone who wanted to start something.*

So Sean stayed where he was, and the vampire came to him.

The man reached the booth, his gaze still locked with Sean's, and then asked, "Pardon me. Would you mind if I sat with you?"

Sean shrugged and gestured to the seat across from him. The vampire nodded and seated himself.

"You are new to this area, are you not?"

Sean grunted. Guy talked a little funny — with speech that had many accents, and yet none — but considering what he was, there was also no telling how old *he was or where he was originally from. "Just got into town tonight. And ye?"*

"I've been here for a short while."

"Mm-hm. And I suppose ye're going to tell me I'm trespassin' on yer territory?"

The vampire cocked his head to the side. "That was not my intention, no. I am, however, curious as to *your* intentions?"

" 'My intentions?' I don't understand ..."

The cook turned around from whatever he had been doing, and gave a little start when he realized that his clientele had doubled without his knowledge. "Oh! Hey,

Mr. Bachman. I didn't hear you come in. You want anything?"

The vampire turned his head slightly toward the cook, but his eyes never left Sean. "Not this time—"

("What else is new?" Sean heard the cook mutter, without true irritation, under his breath.)

"—I merely stopped by to ask you about those donations we had discussed."

"Oh, yeah, the church," the cook nodded. "I'll, uh, I'll check my books and be with ya in a sec, okay?"

"Fine."

"You okay, buddy?" the cook asked Sean.

"Sure. I'll order when ye're ready."

"Thanks. I'll be right back." The cook hustled down to the other end of the counter and dove into a disorganized shoe box of receipts.

The vampire, Bachman, returned his full attention to Sean and continued as though they had never been interrupted. "If you were planning to prey upon this man, lycanthrope, I'm afraid you—"

"Listen, undead," Sean snapped, "if ye're worried I'm stealin' off yer plate, I'll have to suggest ye dine elsewhere tonight. That man's been a bit too friendly for me to leave him to the likes of you."

The vampire regarded him silently for a long moment after that, and Sean still did not scent any indication that he was preparing to take an offensive. Who the hell was this guy?

"You are something of a quandary, my friend," Bachman said at last.

"No more than you are, I'm sure."

The vampire actually smiled a bit at that, and then he did something that stunned Sean Mallory more deeply than any other action the undead creature might have taken.

He offered his hand.

"I am pleased to make your acquaintance, Mister ...?"

"Mallory," Sean answered, not knowing what else to do but accept the offered handshake. "Sean Mallory."

The vampire's smile broadened. "My name is Alistaire Bachman ..."

JOURNEY

THREE

Mark and I bubbled with excitement for *days*. I began working on the plot for the premiere issue, and Mark continued sketching new angles and looks for Alistaire and Sean in their respective vampire and wolf forms. Based on the intensity of the situation — or in Sean's case, the cycle of the moon — we decided that each would have different levels of form and control. If Alistaire were upset, angered, or just getting ready for action, he would "vamp out" to various degrees, so to speak.

The only thing that nagged at me was that, although it probably wouldn't really apply to our introductory story, I couldn't decide on an origin for Alistaire. How exactly did he become a vampire? Why was he so strong willed? If he was created by another vampire, then that vampire should have had tremendous control over him. So what happened?

A great deal of my questions answered themselves the following Thursday night.

I was taking Psychology that semester. I'd originally signed up just to fulfill one of my elective courses, but it had turned out to be a very interesting class. Professor Kullich was a fairly amusing man in his late-forties. The previous week, the professor had first touched on the subject of *hypnotism*. The revelation that we were going to spend the next couple of classes on this *oh-so-mystical* subject evoked mixed reactions from the class, ranging from extreme skepticism to total enthusiasm. I fell into the last group. The chance to learn hypnosis — *real* hypnosis, not the shit they put in the movies — was fascinating, and I figured it'd be the highlight of the course.

That particular Thursday, as I took a seat, Professor Kullich was placing four plastic chairs in a row across the lecture platform. Class began as usual. Then, like a vaudeville showman, Professor Kullich announced that he'd drawn four names at random for a practical demonstration of hypnosis at work, and that anyone who didn't wish to participate should simply say so and he'd pick someone else. I was thrilled when Professor Kullich called my name as the fourth person — he knew I was interested, so looking back on it, I think he probably fixed it for me.

Taking my seat on the end, staring out at the gawking faces with their myriad of expressions, I awaited my turn. Professor Kullich moved from person to person, spending about fifteen minutes with each, and I made a conscious effort to look away and to ignore the soothing, repetitious words until it was my turn. I knew myself too well — if I wasn't careful, my enthusiasm would build and I might want it to work so much that I'd end up faking it after all, both to the class and to myself. I didn't want that. I wanted to be truly, honestly hypnotized.

Finally, the professor came to me. The class had *oohed* and *aahed* at different reactions from the other students on stage with me, but I'd held true to diverting my attention inward or elsewhere. Professor Kullich smiled. "Just relax," he said. "Take slow, deep breaths. Does it bother you to have your shoulders rubbed?"

"Nope," I answered.

He reached up and began lightly massaging my neck over the collar bone. "I want you to pick a spot on my shirt," he instructed. "Any spot, it doesn't matter. But once you've picked a spot, I want you to stare *only* at it. Don't let your eyes roam at all. When you feel like you want to close your eyes, go ahead, but as long as they're open, stare at the *same spot*."

I did as I was told, choosing a black speck just below his Polo emblem. I drew long, deep breaths, feeling relaxed already from the simple act of proper respiration.

Professor Kullich assumed a soft, lulling tone of voice and said, "Now, as you continue to take deep, relaxing breaths, I want you to slowly count down, out loud, from one hundred. Say one number at the end of each, relaxing breath."

I breathed deep. "One hundred, ninety-nine—"

"Slowly," Professor Kullich insisted softly. "Only one number to each breath. Feel the tension flowing from your body."

"Ninety-eight ... ninety-seven ..."

"Relax ..." he continued, "... feel the tension flowing down through your body ... down through your body into your legs ... through your legs into the floor ... relax ... deep breaths..."

I counted down and breathed deep. He lightly rubbed my shoulders and urged me to relax. I don't think I felt anything until I reached about seventy-five or so. I had closed my eyes around eighty-five. I remember thinking absently, just as the number sixty-eight slipped through my increasingly sluggish lips, that I had somehow missed seventy and sixty-nine. I paused for a moment, but Professor Kullich urged me to continue. He later explained that the way to tell when a person is starting to go under is when they either, *a)* miss a number, or *b)* clearly struggle for the next number. I didn't know that at the time, but I had slipped under enough so that I didn't particularly care.

"All right," Professor Kullich whispered, as his hand left my shoulders. "Relax ... deep breaths ... feel yourself relaxing ... keep counting ..."

I was around forty or so when I began jumping numbers so haphazardly that he told me I could stop my countdown. I sat there, breathing deep, waiting for my next instructions.

"I want you — keep breathing ... I want you to imagine that you're at the top of an escalator ... see yourself at the top of the escalator ..."

I pictured myself at the top of the escalators at the local shopping mall, the first moving stairs that I remember seeing as a child. I remembered thinking that the teeth at the bottom would eat my feet unless my mama helped me over them. I smiled slightly in my semi-hypnotic state.

"... now the top of the escalator is where you are now, and the bottom is where you want to be ... very relaxed, with no tension anywhere in your body ..."

In an abstract, ethereal manner, I somehow added this to my image. It's impossible to explain, really, until you do it yourself, but when you get there, it's easy.

"... the top of the escalator is ten ... and the bottom is one ... and as I count down from ten to one, you will see yourself moving down the escalator ... becoming more and more relaxed, feeling all the tension ease from your body ... as I count from ten to one ..."

Breathing deep ... relaxing ... standing at the top now ...

"All right, I want you to see yourself stepping onto the escalator ..."

I did. Now his voice took on a more insistent tone, still soft and soothing, but with more authority.

"Ten, you're going down. You're going down. More relaxed. Completely relaxed, nine, you're going down. You're going down. Down. Relaxed. Feel the tension leaving your body, eight, going down. Going down ..."

As I moved down the escalator, I felt myself truly drifting into some other state. I didn't know what to expect really, but I was much more ... *aware* than I thought I'd be. Instead of going into some sort of "sleep," as the movies always suggested, I found that my thought process actually clicked *up* a notch. I was thinking totally random thoughts, unrelated subjects soaring into, through, and out of my mind in a flash. At first I thought that I must be doing something *wrong*, that I should be concentrating more on what was happening. It felt more like I was entering some dream than anything else. But I soon realized that even as my mind kicked into overdrive, I still heard Professor Kullich's commands, and I still saw myself moving down, down the escalator. Relaxing, no tension, moving down, down ...

"Two, you're moving down, you're almost at the bottom now. Going down. Going down. Totally relaxed. One. You step off at the bottom."

My mind entered a bit of a void at this point, having reached the end of the instruction I had thus far been given. I waited with heightened patience for the next step.

"Now ... I want you to take your right hand and place it over your nose and mouth."

I frowned a bit at this. I felt relaxed; I didn't want to go moving my limbs around now. Still, I did as I was told, bumping my nose slightly on the way up.

"Now ... I want you to imagine that on your right hand, you are wearing a cotton glove. And this cotton glove has been soaked in a very powerful anesthetic. As you take deep, relaxing breaths, you will smell the anesthetic, feel the chemical relaxing you entirely."

As if by magic, I could swear that I smelled alcohol, or something like it, something *chemical*. It made me very loose and relaxed, just as Professor Kullich said it would.

"As you draw deep breaths, I want you to slowly count

down, out loud, from five to one. Say one number at the end of each, relaxing breath."

Deeeeeeeep, relaaaax. "Five." Inhaaalle, exhaaaale. "Four." By the time I got to "one," I felt like a big pile of mush.

"All right, you can lower your hand. Lay it gently on your right thigh."

I did.

"Now ... I want you to think about your right hand. Concentrate on your right hand. Put all your thoughts on your right hand. And as you think about your right hand, you will feel a light, tingling sensation. Very light, very pleasant feeling. Starting in your fingers, working its way up to your palm ..."

Again, as if by magic, I felt it. I noticed it in my thumb first, a little prickle, like it had fallen asleep. Not the sharp needles you sometimes get, just the mild, almost-itchy tickle. This feeling grew according to Professor Kullich's words.

"... past your wrist to your forearm ... all the way to your right elbow. Your right hand is tingling, gently, pleasantly. And as your right hand continues to tingle, it begins to feel very light. Your right hand feels very, very light, and as it feels lighter and lighter, it slowly begins to drift up. Lighter and lighter, higher and higher ..."

It was amazing! My hand actually felt lighter, lighter than air! Any moment it would lift—

Someone's watch alarm went off. A few seconds later, another followed. The students, except for the few actually interested in the demonstration, clamored loudly to their feet, exploding into a bustle of conversation. I didn't exactly come *out* of the hypnotic state, but my hand no longer felt light.

Professor Kullich's voice was next to my ear now, the tone soft but no longer a whisper. "I'm going to count from

one to five. As I count up from one to five, you will become
more aware of your surroundings, more alert. You will
remain physically relaxed, but your mind will sharpen. One,
you're coming up, more and more aware. Two, you're
coming up. Higher and higher ..."

When five arrived, I opened my eyes. The classroom
was almost empty, and Professor Kullich, with his warm
smile, stood next to me.

"Sorry, Neil," he said with a shrug. "We just ran too
long, I guess. Maybe next time, huh?"

*   *   *

Two hours later, I'd plotted the first few pages of *The
Triumvirate*, a Creole woman seeking Alistaire for help
against a voodoo priest. We knew that she found them in the
"North," but we hadn't decided on a city yet. Mark was
working diligently at the kitchen table on his latest
illustration of Sean in "half-wolf " form.

Again, although it wasn't part of the first issue, my mind
kept wandering back to Alistaire's origin. I just couldn't
come up with anything satisfying, and the writer's block was
really driving me nuts.

I needed a break, so I paced into my room to grab a
comic or something. Instead, my hand fell upon my
Psychology book.

"Whatcha readin'?" Mark mumbled, barely glancing up
from his work as I returned.

"Nothin'," I sighed, sitting down across the table from
him. Not really looking for anything in particular, I flipped
the pages back and forth. Whether by coincidence or
subconscious design, I ended up on the chapter on hypnosis,
and a list of the potential advantages of self-hypnotism. I'd
scanned the list before, but I let my eyes dance over it again,

anyway. Improvement of concentration and long-term and short-term memory, boosting self-confidence, stimulation of subconscious creativity ...

I paused, reading that last part over as it caught my eye for the first time.

Stimulation of subconscious creativity ...

"Mark ... hey, Mark," I said, still staring at the key words on the page.

"Mmm?"

"You took Psychology last year, didn't you?"

"Mm-hmm. Got a 'B.' Why?"

"Did your professor cover hypnotism?"

"A little bit. Gave a demonstration one day. Didn't really buy into it myself."

"Do you think you'd remember enough about hypnosis to put *me* under?"

He looked up at me over the rim of his glasses. "Excuse me?"

"I just got an idea." I set the book aside, my chin coming to rest on my thumb and forefinger as I considered my proposition. How much did I really remember about my experience earlier that evening? It *seemed* like I remembered the whole thing.

"Go on," Mark said, a thin trace of impatience seeping through as he shifted focus back to his drawing.

"What would you think if ... well, if we tried to develop these characters by *hypnotizing* ourselves into thinking that we *were* the characters, and then playing Twenty Questions?"

Mark's pencil abruptly ceased its quick motions and he looked up to meet my eyes. "Are you shittin' me?"

I shrugged. "I was part of our class demonstration earlier tonight. And it says in this book that hypnosis can 'stimulate subconscious creativity.' It might give us some interesting ideas by just sitting back and letting our subconscious minds work for us."

Mark dropped the pencil to one side now. "Do you think it ... I mean, would it be *safe*?"

"I don't see why not. According to Professor Kullich, *and* this book, deep down inside, we'd always be aware of who we *really* are. It would just provide us with a vessel for our imagination."

His eyebrows arched at that, and he exhaled through his lips. "What do you need me to do?"

I smiled.

                    *   *   *

"Okay, you can stop counting down now," Mark told me. "Continue to breathe deep, feel yourself relaxing."

I was lying on my living room floor, with Mark sitting on the edge of the couch. I breathed extra deep, forcing myself to lose all tension. I needed total concentration, no distractions, feel the tension releasing, breathe ...

"I want you to imagine yourself," Mark spoke, "floating at the bottom of a warm pool of water ..."

The imagery was all new to me — I'd asked him to play with the metaphors the Professor had used, so I wouldn't tend to get ahead of him. I had no idea of what was next, no way to anticipate his words. I had to truly listen to him.

"The water is the perfect temperature, not too hot, not too cold. *Perfect.* You're able to *breathe* this water. You take this water into your lungs, and it draws the tension from your body, leaving you totally relaxed. No tension can exist in this water."

Breathing deep ... the tension flowing away ...

"You open your eyes, just a little, and you see someone floating on the surface of the water over you."

I couldn't make out much detail — the lights coming

from above cast his features into silhouette — but I knew who it was.

"Slowly, as I count down from five to one, the person will drift lower, drift down toward you. When I say 'one,' he will enter your body. Neil will step aside for a while, and this person will borrow Neil's body. Do you understand?"

I mumbled that I did.

"Five, he's drifting down ..."

By the time Mark reached two, I could already feel something happening. The man above me seemed to reach out in a strange, ethereal way that I can't describe. I felt a presence, alien yet familiar, flowing into me. I believe my breath quickened.

"... he's almost there now. *One.*"

I breathed sharply, the last breath I drew on my own for a while. The duality was overwhelming for a moment, then it passed as I allowed myself to become the passive, the recessive.

I was on the sidelines now.

Alistaire Bachman possessed my body.

Slowly, Alistaire opened his eyes halfway. His head rolled to the side. He saw Mark lean over him, but at first he didn't recognize him. He looked around my apartment. What was this strange place? Where was he?

"Alistaire?" Mark whispered.

Alistaire's gaze shot back to meet his. Mark blinked self-consciously. Even through the haze of hypnosis, Alistaire's eyes possessed a strength that unnerved him.

Clearing his throat, Mark continued. "Alistaire, my name's Mark Hudson. I'm a friend of Neil's. You know who Neil is, right?"

That much he did know. In recent times, when he read in his study or floated through the night air in his mist-form, he had felt a ... *presence* near him. He had been meaning to ask Sean if he had felt anything similar, but for some reason it always slipped his mind.

"Yes," he said through sluggish lips. *"I know who Neil is."*

Mark looked uncomfortable again. The voice was mine, and yet it wasn't. Alistaire maintained his own eyes, and his own voice.

"I'm going to be asking you some questions, Alistaire." Mark again cleared his throat. Alistaire could smell Mark's sweat glands at work, sense his blood flowing faster. The craving reared its ugly head, and, as always, Alistaire mentally beat it into submission. "Some of them might touch on, uh, painful subjects for you, but we'd appreciate it if you told us everything you can. Do you understand?"

The question was unnecessary. What was there to *mis*understand? The mortal was nervous, and that tension was causing a bit of rambling. Still, Alistaire chided himself for his twinge of impatience. If he could maintain infinite tolerance with Trey, then surely he could patronize this young fellow. *"Yes. I understand."*

Mark nodded sharply. "Good," he said. Then he nodded again. Inwardly, Alistaire sighed.

"Okay ... we'd, uh, like to know everything you can tell us about how you became a vampire."

Now it was Alistaire's turn to hesitate. The boy had spoken correctly when he predicted that it would be a touchy subject. " 'How I became a vampire ... ' " he repeated, and then his mind, *my* mind, underwent a drastic change.

My apartment melted away, and shadows consumed us. The carpeted floor gave way to cold, uncompromising stone. Its touch chilled me through my clothes, but Alistaire shrugged it away.

Where are we? I thought.

My home, came the answer. *Five-hundred-twelve years*

ago.

Alistaire rose slowly to his feet. The hypnotic haze still held its grasp, and he swayed slightly when he stood.

"Where are you?" Mark's voice drifted to our ears, from where we could not say.

"Germany," Alistaire mumbled.   Alistaire's eyes adjusted quickly to the dark. A large stairway climbed up into the shadows on our right, and a dark hallway stretched away at our left. The place was bleak and undecorated except for a red banner hanging from the hall in front of us.

Alistaire eyed the banner, and it clearly upset him in some way. Slowly he walked forward, his fingers reaching out to touch the material. The drapery sported an unusual crest on its center. I'd never seen it before, but it vaguely reminded me of the oriental Ying-and-Yang symbol. Alistaire examined it closely for almost a minute before grasping a bunched handful and ripping it from the wall.

"What is it?" Mark's voice echoed from its hidden source. "What do you see?"

"This should not be here," Alistaire stated fiercely. He gripped the material so tightly that it threatened to tear. *"This is not my family crest. He has replaced it with his own."*

"Who?" Mark asked. "Who replaced it?"

Alistaire tugged, and the drape split through the middle, ripping the unwanted symbol in two. He released his grip, and the cloth drifted to the floor. His jaw clenched as he spat the name he hated so much.

"Mikhail."

Again, the world around us changed. We were still in the same manor, but the lighting was now much better and a few scattered personal effects brought more *life* to the home. We stood before a large doorway. A knock drifted from the other side.

Scurrying from a side passage, a short, elderly servant rushed to the door and opened it. On the other side stood a tall man with long, reddish hair. His smile charmed even the air, and strong brown eyes met Alistaire's blues in an instant. In his right hand he held a loose bag.

"Welcome to my home," Alistaire told him.

Odd. Alistaire's voice was different somehow, less ... Wait! That was it! *This* Alistaire was still mortal, still human!

"I thank you, Master Bachman," the man told him. With sweeping grace, he entered the manor.

The man's voice, with the chilling undertone I had just noticed missing in Alistaire's, tipped me off right away that this guy was a vampire. It seemed obvious to me, but Alistaire somehow remained ignorant.

"I've been looking forward to meeting with you, Mikhail," Alistaire said cheerfully. "These plans for the new church sound promising. I wish only to look over them before I commit any funds."

"Of course," Mikhail said with a hint of a smile.

Alistaire gestured them forward, and the servant slipped away. Taking the lead, Alistaire brought them into an elegant dining room, complete with long, stone table and huge hearth. A fire burned away, providing the best lighting so far. The table was bare of any items. Alistaire indicated that the man should lay his plans upon it.

"How long have you been designing cathedrals?" Alistaire asked as the man spread his sheets for inspection.

"Oh, many years," Mikhail answered, that same smile dancing across his features. He stepped back so that Alistaire could examine his work.

Alistaire knew immediately that something was amiss. He was by no means an architect, but these plans were childishly simple, lacking any detail that a true structural design would demand.

"I don't understand," Alistaire said, confusion wrinkling his brow. "Surely these aren't the actual—?"

He glanced over at his guest, and his heart froze. The man's eyes were no longer brown, but a hot, piercing yellow. Alistaire's mouth dropped open, and he felt the urge to scream, but the cry would not come.

"Lord God, help me," he whispered instead.

Mikhail found this very amusing, and emitted a chilling belly laugh. *"No, I don't think so."*

Alistaire turned to flee, but the strength had left his limbs. He stumbled to the floor, and Mikhail descended upon him. He fought to keep his attacker at bay, but this man was no man at all, and a human was no match for a vampire.

Alistaire finally found his scream when Mikhail's teeth broke the skin of his throat, but by then it was too late. His life's blood drained from him, and his breathing came to a halting stop.

Alistaire Bachman was dead.

"Neil?" came Mark's voice, urgency coloring his tone. "Neil, you all right?! *Neil!*"

I opened my eyes. I was lying on the kitchen floor, my arms splayed in front of me to ward off the imagined attack.

"Oh, man. Weird," I said, struggling to get a firm grip on my surroundings.

"No shit!" Mark snapped. "You scared the hell out of me! You stopped *breathing*, man!"

"Really?" I tried to sit up, and that was when I realized that I was still under hypnosis. My vision blurred.

"What? What is it?!" Mark demanded, shaking me slightly.

"I'm still under," I told him.

"I'm going to count you up," he said.

"No, not yet," I heard myself say, and then my recess was over. My apartment again vanished, and Alistaire opened his eyes.

He still lay where he had fallen. The fire had long ago burned itself out. Blood, his blood, stained his shirt in a few spots, but otherwise he saw no telltale mess to indicate what had happened to him. And what exactly *had* happened to him?

He heard a sound to his right, and he sat up. His servant was walking past the doorway to the dining room, his attention fixed straight ahead.

"Franklin!" he called, reaching out to the familiar figure.

Franklin stopped in his tracks. His head turned, and Alistaire drew a sharp breath, his eyes widening in terror. Franklin, the elderly gentlemen who had served him for so long, now stared at him from behind burning, crimson eyes. His mouth parted in a gaping smile, and his teeth peeked through, the hideously large canines cutting his lower lip — his tongue darted out to lick up the droplets of blood. Franklin then looked straight ahead and continued on his way.

Alistaire stared at the empty space where Franklin had stood for several moments longer, a dread understanding dawning on him that his rational mind sought to dismiss as impossible.

"Dear Go—" The blessed Name that he sought to speak raked through his vocal cords like a scalding blade. And as he turned instead to silent prayer, he felt a lancing ache dart through his very mind that caused even more panic than the sight of Franklin's terrifying transformation.

"I have been forsaken," he whispered.

It was at that moment that he felt the call. It came from upstairs, and he knew instantly who it was. It was Mikhail, and he was summoning Alistaire by filthy and heinous means.

He left the dining room on shaky feet, seeking the stairway that would carry him to his destination. At the first step, he heard a scratching noise from behind, and he turned to regard it. A rat scampered along in the darkness, but it stood out to Alistaire like a beacon. He felt a craving rise in him that was completely alien and abhorrent. Was *this* what he had been forsaken to? To become a creature so vile that even the sight of a loathsome *rodent* was enough to mark the craving of his new thirst? Oh, yes, Alistaire knew exactly why he could see the rat in the dark. He'd always dismissed them as legend and myth, but he was never a man given to *denial*, and he knew enough of vampirelore to know that it was the rat's *blood* that called to him from across the room. Was he to be so damned?

As he turned to face the stairway, Alistaire's gaze whisked across the large crucifix hanging proudly in the commons — apparently neither Mikhail, nor Franklin in his new state, had been able to remove it just yet — and Alistaire cringed at the sight of the holy icon.

The call came again.

No! some inner part of himself howled in pain and fear, and the beginning of anger bubbled within Alistaire's breast. Whatever he may have become, he would not tolerate this *blasphemy* in his home!

Through sheer force of will and strength of faith, Alistaire turned back to the crucifix. The likeness of Christ, with His bleeding hands and feet and the crown of thorns driven so tightly down onto His scalp, was sculpted with His head cocked to one side, and He seemed to be looking down upon Alistaire.

Slowly, ever so slowly, Alistaire approached the idol. Pain throbbed behind his eyes, and were he not undead, he would most likely have been perspiring profusely. When he finally stood at the foot of the crucifix, he forced himself down to his knees. His hands trembled pitifully as he brought them up before him, the fingers clasping.

The pulse of the rat's blood beckoned him.

"Enough!" he scolded himself. He would deal with this, this ... foul *need* soon enough.

Alistaire locked his gaze upon the Christ, and though it felt as though his eyes would burst from his head, he refused to let his focus waver in the slightest.

"Our F-Father, Who art in H-H-Heaven ..." he began, and the searing in his throat brought him up short. But he paused only the briefest of moments before swallowing the sting and continuing anew. "Our F-Father, Who art in H-Heaven, hallowed be Thy Name ... Thy Kingdom come, Thy Will be done ... on Earth as it is in H-H-Heaven ..."

And somehow, in someway, although the pain never physically ceased, as he forged on through the Lord's Prayer, he found it easier to continue with every word ...

After a brief eternity of pain and prayer, Alistaire found himself on the second floor, standing before the second room on the right — his study. The call was overwhelmingly strong now, and he opened the door.

Mikhail sat before Alistaire's private hearth, the fire blazing bright. He sat in Alistaire's chair, wearing Alistaire's robe, and reading Alistaire's book. In his hand he held a wine glass, but Alistaire's new, highly acute sense of smell told him that it was not wine that Mikhail drank from that glass.

Mikhail regarded him with a twisted smile. *"So, finally decided to rise and join us, did you?"*

Alistaire heard a footstep behind him, and he did not have to turn to know that Franklin was there.

"I labored for months to find a way for you to invite me into your home, Bachman," he said, sipping again from the

blood in the chalice. *"Franklin was not the owner, and therefore could not invite me himself. That welcome had to come from the master of the house.* You.*"*

Alistaire scrutinized him with raw passion. His indignation reached new heights with each passing second.

Mikhail seemed to know this. He smiled. *"Oh, come now, don't be a fool, Bachman. I am* your *master now. Do not seek to resist. You will only fail, so save yourself the trouble. You will need your strength for the hunt that I will teach you tonight."*

"Never," Alistaire whispered.

Mikhail's smile slipped just a bit. *"I beg your pardon?"*

"Never," Alistaire vowed.

Mikhail snorted, his smile fading away completely now. *"Come to me, you fool."*

Alistaire stood his ground.

Mikhail's expression grew more intense now. He set the chalice aside, and his eyes burned yellow. *"I said, come here,* now!*"*

For a moment, Alistaire felt his resolve slip, but only for a moment. His teeth grew in size, and his eyes glowed white with power that surpassed Mikhail's own. *"And I said* never!*"*

Mikhail hissed and started to rise. Franklin also hissed, and Alistaire heard him take a step forward.

They never stood a chance.

Alistaire came to Mikhail, but not in the way that the invader had desired. Before he could raise his arms to ward off the attack, Alistaire's hands, his nails now long and sharp, closed around Mikhail's throat. His forward momentum carried them both to the floor, with Alistaire landing on top.

Franklin reached them, but before he could assist his vampire lord, Alistaire shot him a look that froze him in place.

"Stand back, Franklin," Alistaire said, *"now."*

"Franklin," Mikhail managed to say, *"I command you to assist me!"*

Franklin stood torn for a few seconds, then it was clear to him exactly *who* was the true authority here. He retreated from the struggle a few steps, then turned and fled.

"Impossible!" Mikhail gasped.

Allowing himself a brief, victorious smirk, Alistaire pulled the pathetic creature to his feet. The vampire did not need to breathe as a mortal would, but Alistaire's grip was so firm that Mikhail was helpless, helpless before this fledgling vampire whom he had created just the night before!

"Because of you," Alistaire spat, *"I cannot pray. Because of you, I cannot speak the name of G— of GOD!"* The Name came out as a scream through the pain of speaking it. Then his voice dropped into an icy strength that caused Mikhail, century-old vampire and terror of the night, to wince. *"But I* shall. *I shall continue to pray. I shall continue to speak to my L-Lord in H-Heaven. I shall continue to read my Bible. And know* this, *you abomination. You have unleashed a* force, *a force the likes of which your kind has never before seen."* He pulled Mikhail an inch closer, and the vampire's yellow eyes revealed an emotion he had not felt for decades — those yellow eyes revealed deep-rooted terror. *"Begone, anathema."*

In one smooth motion, Alistaire thrust the struggling vampire into the fire blazing in the hearth. Mikhail fought to escape, but Alistaire would not let him leave the burning chamber. Eventually the battle ceased, and Mikhail's ashen remains crackled in the flames.

Alistaire stared into the conflagration for some time. His new existence would not be easy, nor would the war he knew he must now undertake. But as he stared into the fire, he took comfort in the knowledge that he had *not*, in fact, been forsaken. He had merely been given a great *task*, like Noah, David, and Moses before him, and he would not shy from it.

First he would claim the life of some wild animal — he must, after all, *survive* if he were to fulfill his mission. And then he would start his new life by pursuing Franklin, and destroying him. A sound snapped his attention to the left. Someone stood before him, and he prepared to attack. He then saw that it was not Franklin. It was someone else, a *boy*. A boy who looked strangely familiar, and yet ... it was *Mark*. Mark Hudson ...

... and I was myself again.

I was in my bedroom now. Mark stood in the doorway, watching me with anticipation in his eyes. I felt no fuzziness, no haze. I was completely out of hypnosis. The scenario was over.

"Well," I observed, trying to make light of my unease. The experience had been both exhilarating and unnerving ... and *tiring*. Not an out-of-breath kind of fatigue, just ... *drained*. "I guess *that* was a success."

"You could say that," Mark said, a grin creeping across his face.

I smiled back.

IV

The echo of her footsteps on the damp pavement created the illusion that someone was following her.

Gayle Matthews shuddered, then steeled herself against the irrational fear. No one *followed* her — she was alone on the empty street — and even if someone did *trail behind* her, she could not allow herself to be detained. She and her people needed help as soon as possible, and her grandmother had insisted that she would find that help here in the North.

At last she reached the address she sought. She tilted her head back and gazed up at the unusually tall and imposing townhouse that awaited her behind the waist-high metal fence. A single light was gleaming from one of the second-story windows. Taking a deep breath, she pushed open the gate.

Timidly lifting the knocker in her hand, she rapped on the door quickly, as though prolonging the act might cause the metal to burn her. Several moments passed without a response, and she felt her resolve slipping. She retreated a few steps just as the door finally opened.

A handsome, rather sensuous white man stood in the doorway. His black T-shirt stretched taut against a better-than-average build, and his pants snuggled tight against his legs. Old-fashioned sideburns accented his dimples when *he flashed her a warm, comforting smile.*

"Need help, missie?" he asked, his masculine voice sporting a noticeable Irish dialect.

"Yes, I ..." She swallowed to wet her dry throat. "I'm looking for a man named 'Alistaire Bachman.' I was told I would find him here."

"Ah," the white man said knowingly. "If ye'll follow me, please."

Gayle blinked in mild surprise. Somehow, she'd half-expected the man to claim ignorance and tell her that she must be mistaken. Instead, he opened the door further to allow her passage, that same, friendly grin gracing his expression. Gayle tugged nervously at her rain coat, then stepped over the threshold into the townhouse.

The interior of the house was well-kept and finely decorated, with high-quality paintings and antique furniture.

"This way, missie," the man said, leading her to a set of stairs. She trailed behind him, her chance to observe the place cut short.

At the top of the stairs, the man turned left and stopped before the second door on the right. He knocked lightly on the old, strong wood, then turned the handle and opened the door without waiting for a reply.

A second white man inside held a book in his hand. He stood in profile before a large bookcase, his head turned slightly to glance at them. He was dressed in a high-dollar suit, which complimented his regal face. He glanced at the man who had greeted her, then rested his penetrating, steel blue eyes directly upon her, and she felt as though his gaze pierced straight into her soul. He parted his lips, and a strong, silky voice greeted her. "Ms. Matthews? I've been expecting you."

Gayle swallowed hard again, and nodded curtly. "Are

you Mr. Bachman?"

The man returned her nod, his movements fluid and graceful. "I am. Alistaire Bachman. Won't you please sit down?" *He replaced the book on the shelf and gestured towards a large, comfortable-looking, leather-upholstered chair.*

"Allow me to take ye coat," the Irishman offered.

She permitted him to slip it from her shoulders and seated herself in the indicated chair. *Alistaire seated himself in his own chair opposite her, and again locked his forceful gaze with hers. She could not help but seize every opportunity to glance away from that stare, so overpowering was his presence.*

"I've been told that you can help me," she began. She tried to relax; it proved to be a futile task. "I'm from the South, near New Orleans. We are a private people, and as such the local authorities tend to view us with a great deal of distrust and skepticism."

"We can identify with that sort of thinkin'," the Irishman chuckled. Alistaire regarded him briefly, a slight smile finding its way to his face. He then turned back to her, although she almost wished that he hadn't.

"My village has been plagued by ..." She hesitated. Would they scoff at her as the police had? Finally, she blurted the words quickly. "By a Voodoo priest, we believe from Haiti."

The Irishman reacted slightly, but it was not a reaction of disbelief — it was born of sobriety. Bachman gave no response.

She pressed on. "This man, this evil man has been drawing people from their homes in the middle of the night. He calls out to them in a way that we cannot understand, and they come to him. The local police will not help us; they will not get involved. My brother, Trey ..." Her emotions momentarily got the best of her, and her throat tightened once more. No, now was not the time! "My brother, Trey, he tried to stop one of our neighbors as he was called away, tried to reach the man before he disappeared into the woods. Trey ran after him, and he ... it seemed as though he fell, but we cannot be certain. His body tumbled into a pit, and he was impaled upon some sort of trap." She sighed sadly. "He died instantly." She regarded her hands for a moment, secretly enjoying the chance to escape Alistaire Bachman's stare, then said, "I have not had time to properly grieve. My grandmother sent me here to find you. She has ways of knowing things, and she claimed I would find a man here, a man from the North who would believe us and try to help us. She says that you *are that man, Mr. Bachman."*

Alistaire mused over her story for a brief moment. He shifted his attention to his companion. "I believe we will be traveling to the South, Sean. Please take Ms. Matthews downstairs and offer her some hot tea while I ready our things." *He faced her once more, and told her,* "We will help you, Ms. Matthews, in every way that we can."

Gayle breathed a sigh of relief, then stood. "Thank you, Mr. Bachman. Thank you very much."

The Irishman smiled and gestured back to the door. "Missie?"

Gayle waited as he opened the door for her, then paused before stepping out of the room. Alistaire Bachman was still seated, his mind focused inward. He sensed her stare and looked up at her.

"If I may ask, Mr. Bachman," she spoke softly. "Who are *you that you can help us? I mean, are you a Voodoo priest yourself? A mage?"*

Alistaire Bachman seemed amused by this, a short chuckle escaping his throat as his head leaned back, turning his face to the ceiling. "Not ..." As he spoke, Gayle looked on in horror as his blue eyes paled into solid whites, and his canine teeth grew noticeably larger, protruding from his lips not unlike a savage tiger or wolf. Despite his lack of pupils, she could not help the feeling that he saw through her more now than ever. The entire change occurred before he could even say, " ... exactly.*"*

FIVE

Mark and I were *walking on air*.

We had tapped into a method of creativity that was *limitless* in its potential. From one small experiment, I was able to shape a clear origin for Alistaire. What was to prevent us from doing the same with Sean, Trey, or any other character, or for that matter, with *every* other character from every future writing or acting project we were part of? If Mark ever had difficulty coming up with a sketch or costume design, a little hypnosis and there it would be. I could access in-depth backgrounds for every character, large or small, that I portrayed on the stage or drafted onto paper. Our own subconscious minds, our natural creativity, had found a way to explore its greatest potential.

Looking back on it, it's unbearably clear that an obsession was forming. Considering that we were basing everything on a single example, our goals and expectations stretched the envelope of ambition, and redefined "going overboard." What did we really know about this new technique we'd invented on a whim? But the details of the night Alistaire was attacked were so complete, so thorough and flushed out ...

Mark slept over that night, and the next day we poured ourselves into the Triumvirate. After some debate, we called our mutual friend, another theatre major named Alex

Monroe, and told him that he just *had* to join us for a little surprise that night (we wanted to "bring out Alistaire," as we came to call it, as soon as we woke, but we decided to wait until after dark — after all, if I thought I was a vampire, then how would I react to the daylight?). Alex was the one person we felt would be open-minded enough not to call the men with the nets, at least not until he'd heard us out.

The hours dragged slowly. The sun was setting at around seven o'clock then, and I found myself counting the minutes. Alex arrived around six, and Mark and I excitedly shared our accounts of the night before. I sensed skepticism mixed with apprehension when Alex questioned us about the process. Not that it mattered — when the sun set, he'd see that the whole thing was very legit, and that there was nothing to worry about!

At long last, the sun crept below the horizon. Anticipation hung in the air — the mood was *electric*. Mark asked if he could try Sean, but Alex just wanted to meet Alistaire. This time I was the one sitting on the couch, while Mark knelt on the floor in front of me and Alex positioned himself on a chair taken from the kitchen table. I wanted to sit upright rather than lie on my back this time, but Mark kept the water scenario much the same as before. Alex held still (not easy for him — his hyperactivity was legendary around the theatre department), making as little noise as possible as Mark counted me down.

I welcomed the floating presence as it merged into my body. A rush of adrenaline pulsed into my veins and my breath caught in my chest. For a brief moment I felt myself next to Alistaire, sharing his space as much as he shared mine, and then I stepped to the sidelines.

He knew even before he opened his eyes that someone other than Mark was in the room with them. He smelled musk cologne and a trace of the same beer he'd seen Sean drink on a few occasions.

"Alistaire?" Mark asked.

Alistaire slowly opened his eyes. He saw Mark on his knees a few feet away, and the new person ... Aaron? no, *Alex* ... sitting beyond him near the balcony doors. The sun only recently dropped beyond the night sky, and he could feel its lingering effect. In another half-hour or so he would be in full form, or at least as close as he could get to it while occupying this mortal's body. The only light came from the kitchen, but he could see as clearly as if every light in the apartment were blazing at full intensity.

He soon noticed that he was seated in a very undignified slump, and he immediately straightened his posture. He crossed his legs and tugged his shirt — another T-shirt? — into a slightly less ruffled state. The sudden, precise movement seemed to unnerve Mark a bit, and Alistaire offered a small smile to reassure him.

Alex leaned forward slightly, his curiosity building rapidly as he witnessed the changes Alistaire affected over my body. He licked his lips and asked, "You're ... your name is Alistaire Bachman, right?"

Alistaire nodded. *"That is correct."*

Mark observed. "You seem more coherent than the last time you ... visited. How do you feel?"

"Fine, thank you," the vampire replied.

"This is unbelievable," Alex remarked. "He's totally different. Even the way he's sitting ... it's not like Neil at all."

Alistaire listened to this quietly, his penetrating gaze drifting away from Alex and around the room. The living room struck familiar cords for him, but in just as many ways it was as if he had never seen any of it before. He saw, smelled, felt everything with incredible detail, minutiae that even he had missed the night before. The plush of the beige carpet, the gummy caulking around the French door windows, the scent of the books on the shelf, the texture of the couch fabric beneath his fingertips, and indeed, the clothing on his body. The ceiling fan whirled about, and he felt the draft against his exposed skin. All familiar, all alien. The compulsion to explore stirred, and before Mark or Alex could react, he rose to his feet and headed for the kitchen.

"Uh, Alistaire?" Mark called uncertainly.

Alistaire chose not to respond for the moment. He knew that they planned on quizzing him about his long existence, and he wanted to acquaint himself with the apartment first. He suspected he would be visiting here with increasing frequency.

To the right of the kitchenette, the walls branched at ninety degrees. On his left, the bathroom. To his right, the bedroom. He walked toward the latter. The scrape of the carpet beneath his sneakered feet coupled with the scratch of the denim jeans between his thighs. He thought idly that sometime he would have to *show me how to dress properly*.

The bedroom wore a distinctly *unwashed* smell, and he knew that it had been some time since *I'd last washed my bed linen*. Nor did he need to open the closet door to know that a pile of dirty laundry waited there in abundance — Alistaire was apparently a bit anal retentive. The spaces between the closed blinds allowed a light from across *my apartment* to filter through, giving him more than enough by which to see.

"Um ... Alistaire?"

Alistaire turned. Mark and Alex stood in the doorway watching him. "Alistaire, would you come back to the living room, please?"

Taking one more moment to gaze about the room, Alistaire nodded and followed the young men back the way he had come. Once back in the living room, he returned to his seat on the couch, the fluidity of the motion bringing him to an almost regal pose. Alex turned his chair around and straddled it backward, and Mark remained standing.

"All right, Alistaire," Mark said, sounding distinctly more relaxed now that he thought he was more in control of things, "Alex and I ... oh, I'm sorry, I haven't introduced you. Alistaire—"

"I know who Alex is," Alistaire told him. He shifted his gaze to the other boy. He then conceded, *"Pleased to meet you."*

"Likewise," Alex returned.

"We'd like to ask you a few questions, Alistaire," Mark continued. "I hope you don't mind."

"I do not."

"Okay." He thought for moment, then shrugged. "I guess the best place to start is to ask you how old you are."

"I was born five-hundred-forty-six years ago," Alistaire told them. Then, anticipating their next question, he added, *"I have been a vampire for five-hundred-twelve of those years."*

"Born in Germany, right?"

Alistaire nodded.

"Wait," Alex said. "Correct me if I'm wrong here, 'cause I've never been good at history, but I thought that 'Germany' wasn't really 'Germany' back then."

"In a manner of speaking, you are correct. However, I cannot stress enough how you must always study your history with great care. History has been rewritten more times than even I can count, depending upon the person or group currently in power. Many thoughts and ideas are said to have originated in one time and region, while they, in fact, spread from somewhere else entirely decades earlier. The German slur term, 'kraut,' for instance, is widely believed to have come about during the first or

second world war, depending upon whom you ask. It has in fact been a favored British slander for us for centuries longer. Trust me when I tell you that I was born in Germany, and it was in fact 'Germany' even then."

Mark spoke up. "So you were ... thirty-four when you were transformed."

"Correct."

"Married?" Alex asked.

"I never took a wife, no."

"Girlfriend?"

Alistaire sensed exactly what that term meant for Alex, and his eyes momentarily hardened so that even Alex was finally unnerved. The moment passed quickly, and he said, *"I courted a few women, but never entered what you would term as a 'real relationship.' That is for marriage, not before."*

Alex pressed on. "So you're against premarital sex."

Alistaire smiled strangely at that, twisting my mouth in a way that felt strange to me. Even from the inside, aware that this was actually *me* responding, I wasn't sure what it meant. He then said, *"Of course. As any true Chr—"* He swallowed, then forced the word through his throat. *"As any true Christ—ian should be. I have seen the rules grow lax over the centuries, of course, and understand that they aren't always taken to heart, even by people I believe to be 'good.' Sean comes to mind as an example. And don't misunderstand me, young sirs — people have* always *violated edict. They are only more open about it today — less hypocritical, if you prefer."* He sighed. *"But it is not my place to judge such things. I only pass sentence on those who blatantly spurn the word of G— of God, and what He stands for."*

Mark and Alex took a moment to absorb this, as did I. I personally didn't think there was anything wrong with premarital sex, believing that this was a taboo taken too literally by the hardnosed Baptists I was raised around. It certainly made Alistaire more complex.

"So you're a five-and-a-half-century-old virgin," Alex concluded with some humor.

"Yes, I am a virgin."

Mark pushed on before any tension could build. "Uh, Alistaire, you say that you were born in Germany, but I notice that you don't have much of an accent ..."

"Sean observed the same when we met. Although I'm never conscious of any change — for it would have been extremely gradual — over the years I have lived in so many locations and among so many dialects and languages, my own speech has worked its way toward neutrality. If you listen carefully, I'm told that every other word does indeed bear a hint of one dialect or another. I'm sure this is also affected by the many different languages I speak."

"How many *do* you speak?"

"German, of course, English, French, Italian, Spanish—"

"I speak French," Alex interjected. "Could you translate something for us?"

"Certainly."

"Le mer est bleu."

Alex and Mark's reactions were remarkably gracious, considering the dumbfounded expression that crossed Alistaire's face. *"I ... apologize,"* he stammered, the closest Alistaire himself had come to unsure ground. *"I'm afraid I did not understand you."*

"I said, 'The sea is blue.' Should I say something else?"

Alistaire shook his head. *"I do not believe that would help ..."* He turned to Mark. *"Neil does not speak French, does he?"*

"Huh-uh," Mark answered, "I don't think so."

"Ah. That must be the explanation, although it is still a bit unnerving.   French is my second language after German; I know it fluently. I should easily understand your words, but as my host cannot, it is as if they cannot reach me, as if there were a barrier between us."

"Interesting."

"Indeed."

"Where are you living now, Alistaire?"

"For the present, I am living with Sean and Trey in Pittsburgh, Pennsylvania. We have a townhouse on the west side of the city. Sean and I moved there three years ago from New York City."

"A townhouse must be expensive. How do you pay the bills?"

"I have made numerous long-term investments over the years that have proven quite profitable. Another of my holdings provides me with a steady supply of blood."

"Really? How is that?"

"I am joint-founder of a non-profit organization which pays citizens for their donations of rare blood or plasma types, then makes this blood or plasma available to research laboratories or to the homes of those who suffer from various blood disorders. This allows these persons or groups to function without an over-dependency upon hospitals or the Red Cross. I claim to have a large family that shares a rare form of hemophilia. The company in Pittsburgh provides me with a continuous supply of blood. Being a significant financial backer spares me any unwanted scrutiny on the matter."

"Have, uh ... have they ever been late getting blood to you?"

"No. And I believe your true question is, 'What would I do if they ever were late getting the blood to me?' "

Alex smirked and shrugged. "Yeah, I guess that's what

I was getting at."

"Blood banks have not always existed, of course, although you would be surprised how far back the concept reaches. And one can always find postmortem blood supplies if one knows where to look. Still, if absolutely necessary, I could survive on the blood of animals for a time."

"Mmm. How long have you known Sean? Where did you meet?"

"We met in New York City seven years ago."

"Did you know that Sean was a werewolf at the time?"

Alistaire smiled at this. *"Yes. Werewolves have a distinctive scent, in both human and meta forms. It is unmistakable."*

Alex asked, "What does it smell like?"

Alistaire smiled again, then even chuckled a bit. *"Well, it doesn't exactly please Sean to hear this, but it reminds me of a wet dog."*

Alex laughed out loud. Mark smiled, then continued, "How did the three of you — you, Sean, and Trey — decide to form the Triumvirate?"

"Sean and I joined forces first. As mundane as it may sound, we simply struck up a conversation in a diner in Manhattan. Sean would say that intuition *played a large role in it — I call it* Divine Providence. *It didn't take us long to realize that we were kindred spirits in our desire to reject the immorality of our cousins."*

"Is Sean religious, too?" Alex asked.

Alistaire opened his mouth to answer, but Mark held up his hand urgently. "Don't answer that, please," he said. "I'm hoping we can have Sean join us later this evening. We'll ask him then."

"I understand," Alistaire said, *"but I'm afraid that probably will not happen tonight. It takes effort to bring me*

here, an effort that I can already feel affecting Neil. It will grow easier in time, but for this evening, I'm afraid that Neil will feel too drained to concentrate on hypnotizing you."

Mark tried unsuccessfully to hide his disappointment. He nodded, then retreated a few steps while Alex continued his inquisition. Even as Mark's enthusiasm slipped for the moment, Alex's grew in leaps and bounds. "You said that you can smell a werewolf in either form. So your senses are that acute?"

"My senses are very acute, though Sean's olfactory is second to none."

"What about other vampires? Can you smell *them*?"

"When it comes to other vampires, it is not so much a question of smell. *The proximity of another vampire triggers what you might call a sixth sense. For instance, if a vampire were anywhere in this apartment complex, I would ..."*

His voice trailed away as his attention shifted. Maybe his olfactory wasn't as powerful or sensitive as Sean's, but he could not help but notice the change in the air. As he concentrated, he immediately identified the familiar "wet dog" scent, and located its source. His eyes focused past Alex and onto Mark, whose back was to them. *"Sean?"*

Alex whipped around, more shaken than he had been the entire evening. Mark stood facing the bookshelf, his respiration heavy through his nose as every breath drew swift and deep ...

"Sean?"

Mark turned slowly, his movement sluggish as one deep in hypnosis. His eyes finally met Alistaire's.

"Sorry to interrupt, Alistaire," he said with an Irish dialect, "but I need ye on the home front. We've got a situation with Trey."

"Understood. Alex, please excuse us."

And with that, like a lightning strike from above, I was back. I shook my head, disoriented by the sudden transition. I was completely out of hypnosis, though drained as before. I could detect no trace of Alistaire.

"Neil?" Mark muttered, his hand heavy on the bookcase for support, the foreign accent gone from his speech. "What the hell was that?"

"Mark? Neil?" Alex stammered, his head pivoting back and forth between us as though he were watching a high-speed tennis match. "What the *fuck* is going on?!"

That's what *I* wanted to know.

VI

Gayle's heart thundered in her chest as she followed the Irishman back down the stairs. Good Lord in Heaven, what had led her to this? What bizarre twist of fate would lead her to seek help against a Voodoo priest ... from a vampire?

"Ye seem distraught, lass," Sean observed as they rounded the bottom of the stairs and walked into the living room.

"I am," she admitted. "My grandmother never said anything about your friend's ... nature.*"*

Sean smiled. "There's a lot about Alistaire that would surprise ye far more than his 'nature,' as ye call it, missie. I've learned to take it in stride, but I suppose that's a bit much to ask of someone who just met him." He gestured broadly to the elegant sofa. "Please, have a seat. I'll have ye some tea in a minute. How do ye take it?"

"Just a little lemon, no sugar, please," Gayle told him as she sat stiffly. He left the room, and she found herself gripping her hands so tightly that her fingernails dug into her palm and her knuckles grew white as the blood drained....

as the blood drained

She shuddered.

Sean returned quickly, and she found herself

surprisingly relieved. The Irishman had a calming effect on her that she welcomed with open arms. Unlike the creature upstairs, who was perfectly cordial but still emanated a strong chill, this man was warm and personable and instantly likeable. His smile was both tranquilizing and sensual at the same time, the realization of which caused her a slight blush.

"Here ye go, missie," Sean said, handing her the cup. Gayle accepted it and sipped at it gingerly. As she savored the pleasant, tasty blend, her eyes wandered to a plaque set upon the coffee table before her. It was beautifully designed, carved from grey-white marble. Across the top, sides, and bottom was Mr. Bachman's first name, although it was spelled two different ways, neither of which matched the one her grandmother had given her. The sides presented it as "ALASDAIR," while the upper and lower margins offered, "ALASTAIR."

In the center of the plaque was the name's history:

"From 17th Century Scotland meaning Defender. He has determined ambitions and is always quick to support. Attractive to females for his show of self-confidence. He builds mountains, and men."

Gayle turned her regard back to Sean, who had been watching her as she read. "It's sort of an inside joke between Alistaire and me," he explained with a sly grin. "We have a running disagreement as to both the proper time and country of origin for his name."

Gayle forced a smile. "You said," she began, unsure of how to breach the subject, "that there was much about Mr. Bachman that would surprise me. Could you share a bit of that with me, please? I must admit that I'm confused that my grandmother would seek help from a ..."

" 'Vampire?' " Sean finished for her. He smiled again,

an infectious grin which spread its way to Gayle's own lips. "Let me put yer fears to rest about that here and now, Ms. Matthews. Alistaire is like no other vampire in the world. He was transformed into the creature that he is over five centuries ago, and in that entire time he has never taken a human life by draining them o' blood. Never."

Gayle still felt uneasy. "But, how can you ... I mean, you say that he's never killed anyone by 'draining their blood.' You didn't say—"

"That he's never killed anyone," Sean again finished. "That's right, I didn't. Alistaire has *killed before. In his fight against those like him, he's been put into a position a time or two when he's had to deal with human servants 'n what have ye, and sometimes he's had to kill. But those people are already forsaken, in one way or another. If I may be so bold, I think it safe t' say that he's never killed a 'good person.' I'm not so arrogant as to say I know for* certain *what a 'good person' is, but that's what I* believe, *missie. And I stand by what I said about his vampirism. He has never bitten a person and drained their blood. He has never taken a victim." He then smiled ironically, and added, "It would be against his nature."*

Gayle felt decidedly more comfortable now. It wasn't so much what Sean said, but the conviction with which he said it. This man clearly held a strong, genuine affection and respect for the vampire upstairs. Gayle knew without a doubt that whatever else was true, Sean considered Alistaire a close friend.

"Tell me more," she urged.

Sean shrugged. "Not much else to tell, actually. He's spent the centuries surviving on whatever blood sources were available. Alistaire is a very holy man, and he loathed what he had become at first. I gather that he destroyed the very vampire who made him on the first night that he arose in his new form, though he's never seen fit to share the details with me — his business, I suppose. Ever since that night, Alistaire has seen it as his God-given mission to thwart n' destroy other vampires."

"But the man plaguing my people is not a vampire," Gayle said. "The few times he's been seen, it's been in the daylight. Why then would Mr. Bachman wish to help us?"

Sean chuckled out loud at that question, then waved his hand to dismiss himself. "I mean no disrespect, Ms. Matthews. It's just that I know Alistaire so well ... Allow me to put it this way: In addition to actin' as a vampire who hunts vampires, Alistaire is probably the world's only undead Christian. An' being such, how do you think his Christian beliefs look upon a pagan practice like Voodoo?"

"I see," Gayle said. It made sense. Just because the man mainly hunted his own kind, that didn't mean that vampires were the only ...

For the first time, it crossed Gayle's mind that Sean knew a great deal about this vampire, apparently lived with this vampire, and would even be joining this vampire when they journeyed home ...

"Mr.—?"

"Mallory is the last name, but please call me Sean."

"Sean, then. May ... may I ask a question about you?" She swallowed hard, not sure if she wanted to know the answer.

"Sure, missie. Ask whatever ye like."

"You obviously serve Mr. Bachman—"

"Oh, I'd hardly say I serve him, lass. After all, who's down here sharin' tea with an attractive young lady, and who's upstairs packing the suitcases?"

Gayle smiled half-heartedly at his joke (and part of her shuddered at the thought of sharing tea with Alistaire Bachman), then pressed on. "Then you obviously hunt with

Mr. Bachman, or assist him in the hunt?"

" 'Hunt with,*' yes. I'm not drivin' by religious beliefs like my friend, although he's expressed more than once how happy it would make him if I 'saw the Light.' I have my own reasons for doing what we do. Let's just call it payin' back some dividends."*

Gayle breathed deep. He said it so casually, with that warm smile. Surely ... surely he wasn't ... "Mr. Mallory ... are *you a vampire, too?"*

Sean openly laughed this time. He then sighed, smiled, and said, "Not exactly."

SEVEN

Spontaneous inventiveness was one thing — spontaneous *hypnosis* was an entirely different matter, and it was a bit *intimidating*, to say the least.

We reasoned that Mark must have wanted to go under so much that he put himself down ... but if that was the case, why did he choose to remain as Sean for so short a time? And why did I break out of my Alistaire mode? Also, if it were that simple to go in and out of the characterizations, why couldn't we just do it at the drop of a hat?

At Alex's persuasion — and he didn't have to try very hard — we agreed to cool our heads for a while. Mark and I continued our work on the comic, but we held back from trying another round of hypnosis. Mark still wanted to try Sean for real the next time, but our hungry drive to explore this new tool of ours had been tempered.

And yet, even as I, quite willingly, backed away from the hypnotic game those several days, I found myself thinking about Alistaire Bachman more and more. I wanted to know him, know all *about* him. What had his long years been like? Was he ever tempted, *really* tempted, to break his vow not to take a victim? Did he ever fall in love, or have a crisis of faith? Did he always win, or had he found a vampire or two that had been more than he could handle? Did he ever develop a long-term *nemesis*?

At one point, I considered asking one of the guys, probably Alex, to assume Alistaire so that I could talk directly to him. But in that same instant, I felt a surprisingly strong wave of possessiveness, almost *jealousy*. I didn't want anyone else to become Alistaire — he was *my* creation, and I didn't want to share. I didn't think about these feelings, didn't consider how odd, and perhaps *unhealthy*, they were. I just ... accepted them.

Objectively speaking, the break was well-timed. My involvement with the main stage shows that semester was thankfully small, for a milestone project loomed ahead of me. Lord only knows what possessed me at the time, but at enrollment I'd decided to take *Producing*, normally intended for graduating seniors, a year early. And unless I wanted to overdo it during finals, it was time to get started on the staging of my selected play.

I had already contacted the local community theatre director, Mrs. Donna Barrett, and proposed the idea of using some of her interns and actors — my university peers were overwhelmed with their own projects. She'd liked the idea, particularly my chosen material. I could have picked a one-act, but I'd decided to go for the gusto — with her assistance, I would co-direct and play Clifford Anderson in Ira Levins' *Deathtrap*.

I arranged to meet Mrs. Barrett and one of her techies, Mike Dalton, on campus at the Old Science Hall theatre. Upon Mrs. Barrett's recommendation, Mike would serve as our Technical Director. According to her, Mike was exceptionally talented, and I was looking forward to meeting him.

As it turned out, Mike and I arrived ahead of Mrs. Barrett, giving us a few minutes to get acquainted. He was a little on the quiet side, though you could see the intelligence in his eyes.

Once Mrs. Barrett showed up, we considered the small space we would have to work with, and she noted a potential problem on the apron. "I'm not sure how you plan to stage everything," she said, "but we've got a dark spot down here."

Mike looked up and observed, "The lighting rails are antiquated."

I paced around the area, thinking. The space was so limited, I didn't want to sacrifice even an inch. I also saw an opportunity to judge just how good our quiet Tech Director really was.

"Mike," I said with a perfectly straightforward tone of voice, "I have three questions."

"All right," he responded in his low but soft voice, waiting patiently for me to continue.

"I *do* want to utilize the full apron. One, can the lights be rearranged to cover this area without messing up anywhere else? Two, if not, is there some way to compensate for it with what we have to work with? And three, just how tall *are* you?"

Without batting an eye, he answered, "No, yes, six-foot-four."

I smiled. *I think I'm going to like working with these people.*

Around lunchtime, we were joined by our Stage Manager, a freshman by the name of Kathy Schaumburg. She wasn't in the theatre department, but she and her brother had helped Mrs. Barrett run crew in the past and enjoyed the theatre's laid-back atmosphere. Mrs. Barrett and Mike went on a food run, leaving us alone. I sat on the front row, quietly trying to figure out just how I was going to cram all the action onto this tiny stage — and mentally kicking myself for taking on this headache in the first place.

"Sorry, not allowed."

Startled, I looked up. Kathy stood before me, her hands

on her hips and a teasingly stern expression on her face.

"Excuse me?"

"You were breaking one of my rules," she informed me. I had absolutely no idea what she was talking about, and my face must have said so. She laughed, a little shrill but not unpleasant giggle. "You were frowning. Sorry, no frowning allowed around me."

Her quirky attitude brought a grin to my lips.

"See!" She pointed in delight. "Isn't that better?"

My smile turned into a laugh, a much-needed tension release. *Now I know I'm going to like working with these people.*

VIII

The mosquitos swarmed the thick, sultry night air outside the town limits. Thousands, millions, of other insects flew and chirped and hopped, painting an evening of pristine nature. Had the occasional electrical light not pierced the darkness, one might have found it possible to forget modern civilization altogether. Few ventured from the imagined safety of their cheap, poorly built homes. When night fell now, it brought more than the moon above. It bore the threat of death, or worse.

The voodoo patriarch cast his arms proudly into the air, as much in symbolic triumph as a part of his ritual. A nude girl struggled before him, her cries reaching only deaf ears as his servants lifted her overhead. With a final gesture from him, they pitched her into the towering bonfire that lit their camp. He laughed aloud as her screams ripped through the night, and he felt the power of her soul coursing through his veins.

Satisfied for the time being, he strode from the fire to his private hut. His servants scampered out of his path, followed by his more slow-witted subjects, those whom he had summoned to his cause from beyond the grave.

The newest of these puppets, stolen from those helpless villagers before proper burial, rested on a bed of spiders. The priest marveled at the sheer size of the dead man, smiling with the knowledge of how powerful such a physique would become with the potency of the undead within him.

It was a simple matter really. The soul of the girl, transformed into arcane energy, ebbed from his fingertips and into the deceased's body. The corpse stirred, then slowly rose to his feet. The priest laughed loudly, dancing about in obscene pleasure.

Staring blankly ahead, oblivious to the sinister spectacle before him, Trey Matthews awaited his first command ...

*   *   *

The large clock on the mantle told them that half-an-hour had passed since the sun dropped below the horizon. Gayle fidgeted anxiously as she and her grandmother awaited Sean and Bachman's arrival. Shortly after landing near New Orleans, the sun began to rise, and the Irishman sent her ahead of them.

"We shouldna move Alistaire during the day, lass," he told her. "Even if we did, he'd be no use until tonight. We'll come soon. Wait for us at yer grandmother's."

"I'll tell you the way," she had said.

"We'll know the way," Sean returned.

Gayle's grandmother was notably less apprehensive than she. The older woman merely rocked in her chair, reading a passage from her Bible in silence. Gayle wished that her calm proved as catching as the Irishman's smile.

A knock sounded against the door, and Gayle nearly leaped out of her sandals. The knock was followed by a voice, Sean's voice. "Ms. Matthews?" he called.

Gayle opened the door, her grandmother rising from her chair to greet the guests. Only Sean stood at the *doorway, with Alistaire visible a few yards behind him.*

"Sean," Gayle met him with a smile.

"Hello, missie," Sean gleamed. "This be yer grandmother, I take it."

The old woman nodded to him. "I thank you for coming."

"We see it as our duty, ma'am," Sean returned cordially. He then added, "Before we come in, I have to ask that ye set aside any crosses or crucifixes ye might have in open sight. Ye don't have to bury *them or nothin', just pull them back a bit, please."*

Gayle hurried to remove the symbols, tokens which her grandmother possessed in abundance — she repressed a shudder against the idea of Alistaire having free entry into the house. But Sean had said just to pull them back, so she indulged herself and left a single brass cross hanging over the mantle.

Alistaire and Sean entered and seated themselves. Gayle offered them tea, but only Sean accepted. While she retreated to prepare three cups, she noticed Alistaire spot the remaining cross, start to look away ... and then force himself to look back at it for several heartbeats. Somehow, that silent moment comforted her.

"... he no longer summons them in their sleep," her grandmother was explaining. "Starting two nights ago, they began openly taking people by force, storming into their homes during the night."

"They grow more confident," *Alistaire said.*

*"Over*confident*," Sean added with resolve.*

"When do they usually come?"

"They've been coming between midnight and three in the morning, mostly," the old woman told him.

"I can sense their presence in the woods to the south of us. It would be too risky to attack them in their stronghold,

even for Sean and myself. But when they come, I will know
it. And then we will act."

*An uneasy silence fell over the room, broken only by the
persistent ticking of the clock.*

* * *

*Little Tina returned to consciousness with a good deal
of pain and disorientation. At first she could make no sense
of her surroundings. She recognized that she was in the
family pickup truck, but things were wrong somehow. And
her side hurt. In a daze, she looked where her Daddy
should have been, but even that was wrong. The cabin light
had come on, so she could see him okay, but he looked like
he was trying to stand in his seat, which he couldn't do
because of his seat belt and the steering wheel. Couldn't he
feel that they were stopping him, that they were in his way?
So why was he still trying—*

*Tina screamed when blood dripped from her Daddy's
nose and fell up instead of down.*

The truck was turned over.

*As Tina struggled, both to stop screaming and to free
herself from the passenger seat belt, memory of the accident
crept back through her clouded mind. They were driving
along one of the back roads. Daddy was driving faster than
usual, trying to get them home before the sun went down.
Mommy and Daddy were always afraid of the sun going
down — at least, they had been* lately *— but they would
never tell her why. She'd heard talk about monsters and
boogeymen from the other kids around the neighborhood,
but Mommy had told her not to listen to them.*

The last thing she remembered was a really loud pop,
*kind of like a balloon, only bigger and louder, and the truck
swerving and Daddy cussing a lot and then a sharp jerk ...*

With a click, the buckle of her seat belt released, dumping Tina against the ceiling of the truck and making her side hurt more. She wanted to scream and cry, but she knew that she had to act like a big girl now. Daddy was hurt and she had to get help.

Moving awkwardly into a squatting position, Tina managed to roll her window open. Her side throbbed as she crawled through the gap onto the damp ground, but she gritted her teeth against the pain. Big girl, *she kept thinking.* I have to act like a big girl.

Standing on shaky legs, she looked all around her, but she couldn't see very much. Everything was dark, and she could only make out one light in the distance. That had to be the way back to the road. How far could they have gone from it, anyway?

At first she planned to walk toward it, but her legs felt weak and she wasn't sure if she would be able to make it by herself — plus the way back looked really dark and scary, and the stories about the monsters that came at night didn't seem so much like stupid little boy talk anymore, no matter what Mommy said. But Daddy needed help, so maybe if she tried calling *for help, just maybe someone would be close enough to hear her. Then she could stay with him and she wouldn't have to walk back by herself.*

"H-Hello?" she called experimentally. "Hello, can anybody hear me?! We need help!" She faced the light directly and let go of the side of the truck so that she could cup both hands around her mouth. "Help! We need help! Can anybody hear me?!"

At first she heard nothing, and her heart sank. Then, when she was about to try again, something that sounded like a voice drifted back to her. Was it just an echo? No, it had taken too long to come back, and besides, it was a deep voice, a grown-up voice, the voice of a man.

"Help! Help me! Can you hear me?! We need help!"

Now she knew that she heard voices. Several voices, all grown-ups. Someone had heard her! They were coming!

Soon she could make out some people heading her way. Her eyes had adjusted to the dark a little, so she could see better now. She counted at least ten men, and they were coming straight toward her. How lucky she was ...

The creepiness of the situation didn't dawn on her at first. In the light of the half-moon, she could see that these men sure were dressed funny. If she didn't know better, she could have sworn that they weren't wearing anything except their underwear, and although she could hear them talking really good now, she couldn't understand anything they were saying. It didn't sound like English at all. She'd heard people around her town speak another language, 'French' if she remembered right, but this didn't sound like that French, either.

The men stood all around her now, but she no longer felt happy about their being here. She felt scared. They stood around her in a circle and kept talking in that funny language, but they were making no effort to help her or Daddy. She felt she had to say something, had to at least try, so she cleared her throat.

Big girl. Have to act like a big girl.

"Uh, we need help," she said softly. Her voice trembled, but she didn't care. "We had an accident. My Daddy's hurt. He's in the truck, stuck upside down in his seat. I think we both need a doctor."

At least one of the men acted like he understood her. He got down on his hands and knees and peered through the driver's side window. Then he pulled on the handle and dragged the door open, scraping a long arch into the dirt.

"Can you help him?" Tina asked.

The man glanced at her, then said something to his

friends. At that moment, Daddy moaned, and Tina felt relieved. The man kneeling by her Daddy touched his throat, then said something more to his friends. A second man reached into the back of his underwear and pulled out a surprisingly long, ugly knife. He threw it to the first man.

"Wait, what are you doing?"

To Tina's absolute horror, the man reached in with the knife and slit her Daddy's throat from one ear to the other. Daddy made a sick gurgling sound and started twitching. Blood splattered thick and fast against the ceiling of the truck.

Tina screamed. She screamed loud.

NINE

Mark and I didn't bring out our characters again until the following Friday.

The evening actually began as a double-date between Mark and me and two young ladies from the dance department named Lora and Alicia. Lora, a Junior modern dance major, and Mark had been casually dating on and off for a month. Alicia, a Junior in ballet, and I had gotten to know each other a few weeks prior. She possessed a bright, cheery personality that I found very attractive — her long, shapely legs, firm breasts, and long, dark hair were just a bonus.

The four of us ate dinner at the Drama/Dance hang-out, a Mexican restaurant called the Mont. Afterward, we decided to buy some beer and wine coolers and return to my apartment. The complex I lived in housed a large number of college students, so a little music and dance on a Friday night were nothing new to the neighbors and landlord.

Outside of motion picture soundtracks, I didn't have much in the way of CDs, so the radio clicked on and the dial rolled to the nearest station of choice. The DJ's Friday night selection consisted mainly of dance music, and Lora and Alicia quickly showed us just how outclassed we were.

Not that we were doing all that badly. Alcohol dashes inhibitions as well as hypnosis, and I soon found Alicia's body against mine, our pelvises grinding together suggestively. We'd yet to really kiss, but I felt damned optimistic about the night to come.

We danced for about half an hour. Mark stepped onto the balcony for a cigarette and Alicia joined him, leaving Lora and me to pour some more drinks. She was about to head back to the living room when she spotted the games at the top of my bookshelf.

"Hey, a Quija board!" she said. "You play that thing much?"

I glanced up at the box wedged between Risk and Monopoly. "Not really. Damn thing never worked for me. You want chip and dip?"

"Huh? Oh, no thanks. I was at a party once where the board predicted a couple would get together. I think those things are cool."

My first impulse was to roll my eyes, but then a notion occurred to me. "Really? You like cool stuff like that?"

"Oh, yeah. So does Alicia."

I smiled. "Then you'll *love* this. Hey, Mark!"

The volume on the stereo dropped and Mark and I explained a little of our recent hypnotic games to the girls. Alicia responded a little skeptically, but Lora expressed strong interest.

"Who would you like to meet?" I asked.

"I wanna meet the werewolf," Lora said. "I like werewolves." Then to Alicia, "Did you ever see 'American Werewolf in Paris?' "

"Fair enough," I said. I socked Mark lightly on the shoulder. "It's been your turn for a while, anyway."

I switched the radio completely off, and the ladies situated themselves on the floor. It took me a while to get Mark under. We all kept cracking up and giggling, and the alcohol in Mark's system made him a little too giddy at first.

Eventually we calmed down enough, and I moved Mark down the numbers, into the pool, and then to the sidelines as Sean floated down into his body.

I noticed a change in Mark's breathing. The air passed heavily through his nose, as it had the previous Friday when Sean made his cameo appearance. I realized that this was not so much a characteristic of *Mark* when hypnotized, but the way that *Sean* breathed.

"Sean?"

Mark's eyes opened, and Sean looked up at me. He smiled. "That's me, lad."

I grinned. Sean sat up from his position on the floor and turned to regard us. He noted the two ladies, then glanced at me with his eyebrows arched.

"Oh, excuse me." As Alistaire, I had known Alex, so I hadn't been sure whether or not Sean would recognize the women. Apparently not. "Sean, this is Lora Kilburn." She nodded to him, a huge grin plastered across her face — *both* women were smiling ear to ear. Whether they thought that Mark was putting on a performance or they believed that he thought he was someone else, they were obviously enjoying the game. "And this is Alicia Stewart. Ladies, Sean Mallory."

"Nice to meet ye, Ms. Kilburn, Ms. Stewart."

"Nice to meet you," they echoed.

"Lora and Alicia are Mark's and my dates for the evening."

"Ye boys have nice taste." He winked at them, and they giggled some more. And then he did something that really surprised me. He squinted a little, then closed his eyes tightly as he reached up to remove Mark's glasses. "Lord, yer friend must have some terrible vision, lad. Lookin' through these is givin' me a headache." He gently handed me the spectacles and continued to rub his eyes.

I stared down blankly at the glasses. They were thick all right, and for a reason. Sean hit it dead center — *Mark* couldn't see three feet without them, which should have meant that, character or not, *Sean* shouldn't have been able to see without them either. Wasn't he, after all, using Mark's body, even from the game's point of view? How could he possibly function without Mark's glasses?

He finally stopped rubbing his eyes. Then he smacked his lips as though trying to rid his mouth of a foul taste and asked me if I had anything to drink.

"What would you like?" I asked him, slipping the glasses into my breast pocket.

"I don't suppose ye have any beer, lad?"

"Normally, no. But tonight is your lucky night."

"I'd like some o' that, then, if you please?"

I stepped into the kitchen and grabbed a can out of the fridge. I could tell it was going to be fun to *watch* the experiment for a change. In seconds, an incredible transformation had taken place. Sean was very different from Mark in many ways. Not just the way he talked, but his facial expressions, his posture, even his hand gestures were notably different.

I returned to the living room with the beer. Sean was chatting away with Lora.

A lot more talkative than Alistaire, I noted.

"Thank ye," he said when I handed him the drink.

"So, Sean," I began, taking a seat on the couch. Alicia moved over to sit in front of me, and I started massaging her shoulders. "Do you know why we've brought you here?"

"I assume ye want to ask a question or two as ye did with Alistaire." He then grew a little more serious. "By the way, lad, I didn't mean to be rude when I called Alistaire home so abruptly last time. Trey was havin' one o' his tantrums, and Alistaire has a way of calming him down."

"Yeah, I wanted to ask—"

Lora interjected, "Who's Trey?"

Sean started to answer her, then hesitated. He looked to me in uncertainty. It took me a second to realize why.

"Oh, it's all right," I assured him. "They know all about the Triumvirate. You can tell her."

He nodded, then said to Lora, "Trey is an intellectually-challenged young man in our charge. Most o' the time, his mentality is about that of a two-year-old, and his temperament tends to be the same."

"When did you first turn into a werewolf?"

"It was around puberty that my ... *differences* started to show up."

"Then you weren't *made* into a werewolf," I observed.

"No, my condition was a gift o' my father's, though I sometimes wish he'd kept the damn thing for himself. It showed up when I was in my early teens."

Lora giggled at this for some reason. Alicia continued to listen, obviously more taken by the story than her friend. Or maybe she'd just had less to drink. She asked, "How old are you, Sean?"

"I'm thirty-six years old, lass," he answered. "Probably about twice yer age."

"Are you immortal, like a vampire, or do you age?"

"Oh, I age, missie. I think I'm holdin' up better than *normal* people, but when it comes right down to it, I'm very mortal. I leave the forever-young stuff to Alistaire. Of course, ye're only as old as ye feel." He winked at Lora.

"Are there other were-creatures in the world?" Alicia pressed on.

"Ye mean lycanthropes that turn into animals *other* than wolves?" Alicia nodded. "I don't for sure. For myself, I've never met lycanthropes other than werewolves, but that doesn't mean they aren't out there. I heard a theory that it depends on the native region of the man infected. For instance, I did once *hear* of a man in India who could turn himself into a tiger. Was he a true lycanthrope? Who knows? Neil, do ye think I could have another beer, please?"

"Sure." I hopped up, took his empty can, and headed for the kitchen.

I was glad Lora and I had struck up that opening conversation about "cool stuff." This session, despite guests, alcohol, and the generally party atmosphere, was turning out to be the best one yet. Our apprehension over the whole matter seemed almost silly now. It was all so incredibly interesting. Sean was a *great deal* more talkative than Alistaire, and I was tempted to hunt up my tape recorder in case I should miss anything important. Where in his subconscious had Mark given birth to Sean? Was he imitating someone from his past, or was this an entirely new personality? Then again, how could I hope to answer these questions about Sean when I hadn't the first clue to the same answers concerning Alistaire?

When I returned to the living room, Alicia was again asking a pointed question while Lora snickered into her wine cooler. "... so during most days, you're only able to change into a 'wolf-man,' but during the three days of the full moon, you can turn into an all-out wolf? Does the full moon at night send you out of control?"

" 'Out of control' is puttin' it a bit nicely, I'm afraid," Sean said with a sigh. "During the three nights of the full moon, I couldn't hold human form even if I had enough sense left to *try*. I curb my bestial rages at other times, but on those three nights, I'm as out of control as ol' Lon Chaney himself."

"And that's when you lock yourself away," I interjected softly, pushing him toward a specific area Mark and I wanted to learn about.

Sean nodded. "Aye. Thanks." He took the beer. "Currently, I use the basement of our townhouse in Pittsburgh. It's bolted and barricaded thoroughly, and I also count on Alistaire and Trey to contain me if I ever happen to get loose."

"You ever gotten loose?" Lora asked.

Sean hesitated for a moment, then said, "Not since I've been with Alistaire, no," and followed it with a quick swig of beer, which suggested to me that he'd rather not elaborate further, at least not at the moment. Then he suddenly froze, and his hand went to his face to stifle one sneeze, then another. "Do me a favor, would ye, Neil, and say somethin' to Mark about his smokin' habit?"

I laughed. "I'll do that."

"Hey now," Alicia said with mock irritation. "Let's not start in on smokers." She pointed an accusing finger at Lora for emphasis.

"I don't mean to preach, missie," Sean threw in quickly. "It's just that cigarettes play havoc on my sense o' smell as it is, and the stench is *all over* Mark. I'm extra grateful for this beer just so I can keep the *taste* from overwhelmin' me."

I sat down behind Alicia once more and resumed her neck massage. She leaned back, this time more comfortably than before. Her arms settled up on my knees and her hands began gently caressing my shins. A stirring in my groin reminded me that I had hopes for this evening that had nothing to do with vampires or werewolves.

"Sean," Alicia said, "you said that you inherited your condition from your father. Tell us more about your family. Are your parents still alive? Any brothers, sisters?"

"My mother died when I was very young. I'm sorry to say that I don't really remember her that much. My father was a good enough man, but he tended to disappear on us frequently, sometimes for days at a time. I didn't understand why then, although the reasons are obvious now. By the time I was eight years old, my sister and I were taken in by foster parents."

"So you have a sister," I confirmed.

"Older sister, yes."

"That's good to know, especially now that you've verified that you inherited your lycanthropy from your father. Mark and I had discussed the possibility of your siblings being similarly—"

"My sister is not a werewolf."

The sudden harshness in his voice stunned me into silence. I felt tension creep back into Alicia's shoulders. Even Lora's non-stop giggle caught short for a moment. Sean sat rigid, his face tight, his hands clenched into fists, his eyes not quite meeting ours. I found myself speechless — such abrupt hostility I would have expected from *Alistaire* before hearing it from the laid-back Sean Mallory.

For a moment we sat in silence. Then Lora's dauntless titter returned — for what new reason, only God knew. Sean rose from his place on the floor.

"I don't mean t'be rude. I just don't feel like talkin' anymore." His words were cordial enough, but his tone distinctively stated *don't-push-me.* He swallowed another gulp of beer, sighed heavily, then asked, "All right if I step out onto the balcony for a short bit? I'd like a breath o' fresh air, if I may."

I gestured toward the French doors and Sean moved outside. Lora rose and casually followed him. I started to tell her to give him some space, but then thought better of it. Maybe her flirtatious manner would improve his mood. If he wanted to be alone, I was now confident that he'd say so.

"Was it me," Alicia asked, her voice a bit softer than necessary, "or did Sean kind of ... *overreact* just now?"

I half-shrugged. "Your guess is as good as mine. Mark

and I have discussed Sean's disposition at length. I've even plotted it through half of our first issue now. But I've never 'met' Sean before tonight. I don't really know as much about him as I do Alistaire."

Alicia nodded. I was glad that she was treating this all much more seriously than her friend. I really liked Alicia, and I was glad to be able to share our recent explorations with her, and not have them taken for granted or treated as foolish. She obviously understood why we found them so fascinating, but was equally clear that it was ultimately just a *game*, and nothing to find alarming or intimidating.

"You're going along with this a little better than Lora," I pointed out.

"I think she's a little more nervous about this whole thing than she's letting on. Add the fact that she's pretty drunk, and we get the giggle machine."

I smiled. I shifted my hands a little higher on her neck. "How's that?"

"Mmm. Feels good." She finished off the last of her wine cooler.

"Want another one?" I asked.

She thought about it for a second. "No, I'd better not. It's pretty obvious who's going to be doing the driving tonight."

"You know," I hazarded, "you *could* just stay here tonight."

"Oh, really?" she responded coyly. "And what exactly would the sleeping arrangements be?"

"Well," I returned, matching her tone, "I suppose you and Lora could take my room and Mark and I could crash in here."

"Or?" she prompted.

"Or," I continued, "we use the same two rooms, but change the pairing up a little bit."

She now turned to face me. Her right elbow came to rest over my groin, and applied a gentle pressure in that region. Her shirt, which she'd worn buttoned low for a majority of the evening, twisted in such a manner that I was afforded a nice peek at her cleavage. She noted the momentary drift in my glance, and her response was a sultry smile.

The gears had officially shifted.

"Mr. Carpenter," she asked, "are you making a pass at me?"

"I thought we covered that much when I asked you out."

"True," she admitted. "I'll rephrase the question." Her voice lowered to a conspiratorial whisper. "Are you trying to *fuck* me?"

I whispered back, "*Yes.*"

"Good. But I hope you're into safe sex."

"Absolutely."

"Do you have any condoms?"

"Uh-huh."

"Good. Then we won't have to ask Lora for any."

She turned completely around and rose to her knees and I leaned forward to meet her. We'd tossed a few pecks back and forth before, but this was the first time we really kissed. She was good at it, too. Her tongue darted into my mouth with considerable force and her hands rose to the back of my head to ensure that I couldn't retreat ... not that I had any such intentions, mind you. With one hand I matched her maneuver to the back of her neck, while the other crept down into the alluring valley of her breasts. They were as firm as I'd anticipated, and it was obvious that she wore a brazier for etiquette rather than necessity. Nope, I didn't plan on escaping anywhere.

After a few heated moments, it was Alicia who pulled back. "Before we get going, don't you think we should do something about your friend?"

"Why?" I asked, trying to resume our kiss. "Isn't Lora interested in Mark?"

"She is, but I wasn't referring to Mark. I was talking about Sean."

I blinked stupidly for an instant. In my quick fervor, the hypnosis session had conveniently slipped my mind. "Oh, yeah. I guess I shouldn't leave the werewolf on the prowl, huh?"

She laughed. "Probably not."

I kissed her quickly, then stood. "Don't go away."

She rose with me. "I think I'll wait in your bedroom."

With an audible groan, I moved away from her and quietly opened the French doors, forming in my mind the exact words I'd use to explain to Sean his quick dismissal. I then found my concerns unnecessary.

Outside on the balcony, Mark — make that *Sean* — and Lora were twisted in their own embrace of lust. Lora's halter top was down around her waist, and she was kissing the back of Sean's neck while the "older" man sucked feverishly on her breasts.

For a minute the objective, clinical side of me kicked back into the front lines. What should I do? I didn't want to interrupt them any more than *I* would want an intrusion, but should I just leave them, leave *Mark*, as they were? Did Lora truly comprehend that Sean was really just a *character*? How would things go later when Mark was just Mark, with a full recollection of everything that had happened but acting nothing at all like Sean?

In the end, courtesy won out, and I decided that I'd mind my own business. Mark could work things out later in whatever manner he saw fit. Maybe *Sean* and Lora would end up dating. After all, Sean was merely an extension of Mark himself, and even the younger version of the two was mature enough to deal with his own sex life.

Besides, *my* hormones were screaming for attention.

Closing the doors quietly, I removed Mark's glasses from my pocket and placed them on the kitchen table, turned out all the lights but a single lamp in the living room, and headed for my bedroom. The door stood open a crack, and I slipped inside and shut it behind me.

Alicia lay on my bed, still clothed but minus her shoes and with her top unbuttoned all the way to the bottom. I grinned and crept toward her, losing my own shoes along the way. The only light was my small desktop lamp-clock, but she still appeared radiant to me, almost as if she were glowing.

"That was quick," she observed.

I grunted.

"Condoms?" she asked as I reached the side of the bed.

I answered by sliding open the top drawer of my night stand and producing a box of Trojans. Holding it in one hand, I used my thumbnail to tear through the perforated arch along the backside and open its top, spilling the contents.

Satisfied, Alicia pulled me down and resumed our kiss. I lay down, half on top and half to the side of her, enough to allow my hand to return to its earlier pleasantries. Her nipples strained against the material of her bra. The clasp was in the front, so I quickly relieved them of their confinement.

Our breath was coming faster and heavier now, and she tugged at my shirt. I rose long enough to lift it over my head while she discarded her own shirt and open bra. Now mutually topless, I enjoyed the sensation of her bare flesh against mine, the warm and velvety smoothness against my chest and neck and under my gripping hands. I shifted my mouth down to her throat. She gasped as I chewed lightly on the side of her neck and up to her earlobes.

"Harder," she breathed. I complied, now including the sides of her ears and on down to her shoulders in my non-stop sweep. I danced around to her front and licked and chewed at her left nipple.

Uttering a heated growl, she shoved me back onto my haunches and clawed at my belt. This time we undressed each other, our bottoms joining our tops in the growing heap on the floor. We didn't linger at the underwear and were swift to break down to our birthday suits. She pushed me over so that she could now lay on top of me. Her loins grinded energetically against mine, exciting me into reciprocating her animalistic grunts. This continued for a few minutes before she finally reached for a condom. She ripped the wrapper away with her teeth and rolled the latex over me with seductive strokes.

"Enough foreplay," she mumbled.

Pinning me at the shoulders, she used me for stimulation before leaning back and impaling herself. In almost humorous afterthought, she reached out and turned off the light. I could still see her outline in the streetlight coming through the blinds, and my hands continued to trace the muscles of her legs, toned and shaped from a lifetime of dance. I could smell tobacco and her sweat as it crept from her pores, could feel the heat radiating from her skin, could hear the building intensity of her pounding heart, as if my sexual exhilaration was bleeding into a heightening of my senses.

Her head hung back as she rode me toward her first orgasm. I shook in sensual delirium, not from the motions of her pelvis, but from the beautiful glow of her exposed neck. Her heartbeat pounded louder and louder, and even in the dim lighting I could make out the subtle rise and fall of her pulsing jugular. My tongue, swollen as if from thirst, darted forward to wet my lips. Her grip tightened on my shoulders as she delivered a long, guttural moan. When she relaxed, I rolled her over so that I could now drive forward. She posed no argument, but lifted her legs until they wrapped around the small of my back.

I thrust into her savagely, hooking my arms under her back and bracing her against me. She moaned with each drive, eager for my feral assault. I kissed first her eyelids, then her mouth, then her chin, and finally her throat. I whimpered, not due to coital pleasure, but at the ecstacy of her blood racing beneath the surface of the oh-so-delicate tissue. Tentatively, like a virgin boy touching breasts for the first time, I opened my mouth wider and bit down on her neck.

She moaned louder. "Harder," she demanded.

I applied more pressure, my eyes rolling back in their sockets as I began to tremble.

She whispered, "Oh, yes. More."

A grin slowly spread across my lips, distorted wickedly by my open mouth, and I gave her more.

"Now move faster," she commanded.

I ignored that particular order. If anything, my thrusts slowed as my jaws tightened.

That was when she made her first sounds of discomfort. "Ow ... mmm, Neil, honey, if you're going to bite that hard, you'd better keep fu—"

With sudden brutality, I slammed into her with the entire force of my hips and bit her throat with all my strength. My canines pierced her flesh like twin needles. They didn't go very deep, but the holes they made were surprisingly clean. I came nowhere near her arteries, but I drew blood, and I sucked it from her as if my entire existence depended upon it. Alicia cried out, but not from simple pain. As I sucked at the wounds in her neck, I added newfound vigor to my pounding against her hips, and she thrashed about under the power of an orgasm that dwarfed her previous tremor. I gave no quarter, but continued to hammer her into the mattress, and her rapture soon overwhelmed any awareness of what I was doing to her throat.

*   *   *

Sunlight burned through my open blinds, waking me with unwanted torment. I squinted against it and rolled away.

Alicia sat on the edge of the bed, pulling on her pants.

"Hey," I said with a smile.

She jumped, blinking over her shoulder at me as if I had screamed at her.

"Sorry. Didn't mean t'scare ya."

"I ... I didn't know you were awake yet."

"Sun woke me." I glanced at the clock. It was early. The sun had probably just cleared the top of the apartment building opposite my window. "Why ya leavin' so soon?"

"I ... have a recital meeting today. I need to go home and change before it starts."

Only then did I notice how rattled she seemed. Her hands trembled slightly as she pulled on her shirt.

"Alicia, you all right?"

"I'm fine," she insisted a little too quickly.

"You sure?"

"I'm sure." She finally slowed down and turned my way, barely. She seemed afraid to face me. "Neil, we can't see each other again. Not like this."

Now I was the one surprised. "What? Why?"

"I ... I just ... don't get me wrong, okay? You're a really great guy and all, and the ... the sex last night was incredible, in its own way ..."

In its own way? What was *that* supposed to mean? I was completely dazed. It hadn't occurred to me that I was a one-night stand to her. Great sex aside, I honestly liked her, wanted to get to know her better. Everything had gone so wonderful the night before ... at least I *thought* it had. "I don't understand. Alicia, if something ..."

"Look, I'm not trying to be mean, Neil. I won't say anything to anyone else. I'll cover this up until it's healed, so no one'll think ... whatever. I won't give you the cold shoulder or anything. Maybe we can even go out again sometime. I just don't want to get serious, okay? This has been ... it's too much for me. I'm sorry."

"Alicia—"

She stood, slipped on her shoes, and headed for the door. "I'll leave Lora here for now. She and Mark or Sean or whoever he is are still curled up on the couch, and I think they'll probably need some recovery time. I'll talk to you later, okay?"

She left, leaving me completely baffled. I truthfully had *no* idea what had gone wrong. I sat still on my bed for a long time, trying to make sense of it all.

My confusion was legitimate. I remembered only a night of fun and hot, passionate sex. Until this very writing, as I sit here recording these memories onto paper, I had absolutely no recollection of the change that had occurred in me.

Or the bite.

X

The voodoo acolyte smiled at the gratifying sensation of the man's throat tearing beneath his blade. His patriarch allowed him the pleasure only on occasion, preferring to hoard the souls for himself. The acolyte learned quickly that opportunities presented themselves to those who showed initiative.

The little girl kept screaming, and though he knew no one would dare come to her assistance at night, he didn't particularly feel like listening to the shrill wail. He barked an order and one of his aides rushed to cover her mouth. Despite his indulgence with the adult male, he prided himself that he would indeed have the best of both worlds, and would return to his patriarch with a child-offering that would surely keep him within his master's continued favor.

Ordering a return to their encampment, the acolyte spoke only a few words before a low hiss drew his attention to the darkness surrounding them. The others heard the sound as well, and more than one drew their knives, their eyes darting back and forth.

A mist swirled in from above them. The acolyte called for a protective ring and uttered a few words of defense, but his concentration was lax, his composure unsettled. He held his dagger high, the man's fresh blood running down the blade and onto his hand. The girl's mouth was *uncovered and her hysterical cries again filled the air.*

Then her screams were joined by the necromancers'.

In a flash too swift for the naked eye to follow, the mist solidified, and Alistaire Bachman descended upon the group.

Their talismans and wards proved utterly useless as the vampire raged through them. His teeth glistened and his eyes blazed in white fury as he smashed and ripped and slashed and disemboweled the heathens with brutal efficiency. A few of them managed to clip their blades at him before he ended their pagan lives, but it would clearly be only a matter of time before he exterminated the lot.

The girl witnessed none of the carnage erupting around her. Her attention had never wavered from the limp form of her father, now beyond any help she could hope to find for him. She crawled to the open door of the truck and clutched at his hand. She didn't even respond when someone tried to pull her away, but held onto her dead parent with determination.

"I guess ye were right after all, Gayle," Sean admitted as he stepped away from the shattered child. "We do need ye. Ye'd best try to drag her away."

Gayle moved into his place, whispering small words of comfort to the girl as she pulled gently at her shoulders, wishing futilely that the horrified cries of the voodoo disciples, and Alistaire's animalistic snarls, weren't so unbearably near.

Sean scanned the area. His senses told him that the dozen or so men they'd found near the overturned truck were but a few of many in the area, and it would only be a matter of minutes or seconds before reinforcements arrived. If it were just he and Alistaire he'd have no worry, but there was the little girl to think of, and Gayle, who'd insisted on coming when Alistaire announced that a child was in jeopardy. Should he help his partner now, or ...

Gayle finally managed to separate the little girl from the man in the truck, whom she assumed to be the girl's father. She took the child into her arms, hoping the offer of protection would give her some comfort, and turned to face Sean. Her eyes widened as more of the briefly clad men emerged from the thicket, one of them brandishing a hatchet and charging at Sean from behind.

"Sean!" she cried.

The Irishman was already spinning on his heel before her warning was finished, his face contorting in rage as he faced his would-be assailant. Then Gayle's relief transformed into shock at his next move.

The muscles in Sean's right arm, from fingertips to shoulder, rippled and bulged. Thick, brown hair emerged from his exposed skin. His fist changed into a hybrid of human hand and padded, animal paw, and claws that rivaled Alistaire's extended into plain view. With a slash of iron-like strength and power, Sean cleaved a gaping wound down the man's throat and chest.

Gayle gaped in astonishment, now clutching the girl to her with her own need for solace. Sean glanced over his shoulder at her, and she could already see the change taking place in his face as well. His sideburns, previously dark and lush, grew thicker. The hair atop his head grew longer, his ears pointed, and his teeth seemed ready to burst from a mouth too small, although his jaws were already lengthening to accommodate them.

"Stay back!" he commanded in a barely human voice.

Now Gayle understood how Alistaire Bachman, who was not exactly a mage, and Sean Mallory, who was not exactly a vampire, waged their war together.

The werewolf leaped forward, diving into the new wave of attackers with the same vigor as his partner. The voodoo underlings stood no chance in the face of their twin fury, but they fought on anyway, preferring to face death now than whatever punishment their master would dispense for failure.

The fight was nearing an end when another group joined the last, and this time there was a notable difference. The vampire and werewolf's blows and bites did not affect them quite the same. The new opponents sported an unexpected strength that even allowed one of them to knock Alistaire from his feet. Suddenly, the sway of the battle was no longer certain.

Gayle yelped in surprise and terror as a rough pair of hands seized her from behind. A sickening stink of rot and decay overwhelmed her as she felt herself and the girl in her arms lifted into the air and unceremoniously tossed over a massive shoulder. She twisted in a futile resistance, trying to squirm her way free, calling for Sean to help her. Her abductor glanced back at her in mute curiosity. Gayle froze when she glimpsed that blank, emotionless face.

"Trey?" she whispered when she recognized her deceased brother. "Oh, my God! Trey! Oh, God, Trey, what have they done to you?!"

The creature that had been Trey Matthews offered no answers as it continued its journey into the dense woods, leaving the vampire and werewolf to fight on, unaware for the moment that those they defended had been spirited away.

*   *   *

The patriarch was not pleased to learn that unknown, supernatural creatures were loose in his woods. They could only be strangers to his domain, for no such beings could have eluded his attention for long. Whether or not they *intended to threaten his position he did not know, but they had already attempted to thwart his underlings in their given task, and that was provocation enough. He would use the new sacrifices, the girl-child and young woman, to increase his potency, and then he would go into the woods himself and destroy them.*

The woman continued her pleas, which came as no surprise from a new victim, but he observed that she directed all of her cries to his latest slave. Apparently they had been related. No matter, his slaves were mindless and under his complete control — the woman would receive no assistance from her dear, departed sibling. In a few minutes, she would be no more, and her brother would aid him in his termination of the vampire and lycanthrope.

Gayle, stripped, bound, and helpless in the grasps of the undead monsters on either side of her, could not hear the patriarch's confident thoughts, but her own fears were beginning to echo them. Not far away, the little girl lay in deep shock as she was also prepared for this wicked ritual. As hard as Gayle tried, she could not even get Trey's attention, much less his help. He stared with milky, clouded eyes into the heart of the blazing inferno in the center of the camp, not even a hint of humanity in his expression, but she couldn't bring herself to simply give up. She had to reach him! Her very life depended upon it!

Unfortunately, she was out of time.

The patriarch gestured, and the zombies lifted her over their heads and stepped toward the flames. She screamed and struggled half-heartedly, but she knew that it was hopeless. She was about to die.

Suddenly a howling roar filled the air, and a tremendous crash sounded from the rear of the encampment. More annoyed than concerned, the patriarch turned to regard the source of the interruption. Gayle twisted around as best she could.

Wading through mindless zombies and godless vassals, Alistaire and Sean burst onto the scene. Their ferocity and commitment to the battle was untempered now, and each released the full force of their nature. Sean bit and mauled his opponents in his full, enormous wolf-form, standing nearly as tall on all fours as the upright men around him. Alistaire appeared only marginally more human, his fangs and facial features distorted with pure ... Gayle could find no other word to describe it but vampirism, *the former cut and noble visage replaced by demonic horror. She did not withdraw from it, but prayed that the vampire's power would serve him* now *as it had throughout his centuries-long war.*

The patriarch's eyes narrowed in anger, and he turned back to the matters at hand. He cast a look toward Trey and ordered, "Dispose of them. Now." The zombies bearing Gayle took another step forward.

Throwing aside his latest adversary, Sean Mallory leaped forward and broke the circle of thralls, his teeth bared and ready to dismember Gayle's captors. The moment before Sean could act, Trey moved in and smashed the wolf across the side of his large, canine head. The werewolf yelped and rolled away from the blow, barely avoiding the fires as he tumbled.

Then Alistaire seized his chance to act. His body again dissipated into mist form, and the supernatural cloud swirled through the air toward Gayle. This time the patriarch interfered, muttering unintelligible words under his breath and casting a glittery powder through the air. The powder hit Alistaire's mist-form like a physical force, and the vampire found himself struggling not to lose total cohesion and drift away on the wind.

"Enough of this!" the patriarch order. "Cast her in!

Now!"

The zombies lifted Gayle high over their heads. With sentimental fatalism, Gayle looked to her brother. "Goodbye, Hercules," she said, her words almost too soft to hear.

That nickname, the name young Gayle had called her older brother when his inevitable size became apparent at puberty, the name she hadn't called him for years, bore a greater impact on the creature that had once been Trey Matthews than any of her earlier cries for help. The large zombie's eyes shifted to finally look at her, powerless, exposed, and about to die a terrible death. The zombie saw her for the first time, and a flood of memories from his previous life surged through his mind with dizzying force. He blinked and shook his head.

"Now!" the patriarch repeated, his eyes fixed on the swiftly recovering werewolf. "Cast her in now!"

As the two zombies craned their arms back to pitch their burden, Trey dove forward and seized their arms. They hesitated, their mental capacities insufficient to grasp such concepts as betrayal. Trey twisted and they released his sister, dropping her roughly onto the ground behind them. He then turned around and cast the two of them into the flames in her place.

"No!" the patriarch bellowed, feeling his power diminish rather than grow. He faced his former slave, contempt causing him to tremble uncontrollably. "How dare you?! I'll dispatch your eternal soul to the pit of hell!"

Evidently unimpressed with the threat, Trey advanced upon him. The priest waved his arms in a wide gesture and energy crackled from his eyes, striking the zombie full in the chest and knocking him from his feet.

As he prepared to cast another spell that would transform the zombie into a puddle of organic goo, the patriarch failed to notice the shape forming from the mists behind him. The vampire stepped forward and closed a vice grip around the man's throat. The priest struggled for breath, clawing futilely at the vampire's crushing fingers, then dropping a hand to his side, trying to reach for something strapped to his leg.

"Savage infidel," *Alistaire spat in disgust.* "You embody all that is twisted and evil in this world. You are not some pathetic creature cursed against his will. You chose this path, this life, away from the word of G— word of God, and now you shall—"

The vampire's heartfelt words fell short as the patriarch grasped the blade sheathed in his human-leather boot. The silver dagger lashed out, slicing a deep cut along Alistaire's side. Cursing himself for his self-righteous delay, the vampire released his hold on the man's throat and stumbled back in pain. Sean, his head finally clearing from Trey's unexpected belt to his temple, snarled threateningly, but his stomach knotted in dread of challenging the deadly metal, and the priest knew it. Brandishing the weapon, he leaped forward to follow through with his attack on the vampire.

He never reached the undead German. A huge, black hand closed on his wrist and wrenched hard until the dagger dropped to the ground. Then Trey Matthews lifted the stunned voodoo priest over his head and cast him into the ever-waiting bonfire.

The large zombie stared into the flames as his former master burned and thrashed in agony, then turned and went to his fallen sister. He knelt beside her, stroking the side of her head as she looked up at him with uncertainty.

"Trey?" *she whispered.*

The zombie opened his mouth and returned, "G ... G— G— Gaaayylle ..."

*   *   *

"Ready to leave when ye are, Alistaire," Sean said as he returned from checking their chartered jet. "Non-stop overnight to Pittsburgh."

The vampire smiled, a trait that Gayle had seen with increasing frequency over the last few nights. She knew this vampire, this man, much better now, and she appreciated him for what he was.

"You had better say goodbye to your sister, Trey," *he said soothingly.* "We have to leave now."

The large man nodded with slow but solid understanding and turned to Gayle. "Bye-bye, Gayle," *he told her. He gave her a little hug, careful not to squeeze her too hard.* "You come visit me soon?"

"Yes, Hercules," she answered. She'd called him by that name more in the last three days than she had in the last ten years. "I'll come see you soon. And I'll tell Grandma that you said goodbye, too."

Trey nodded again and released her. Sean took him by the hand, offered Gayle a warm smile and wink, and led the large man to the waiting plane.

"I want to thank you one last time, Mr. Bachman," she said, her eyes following her brother as he ambled away. "Not just for saving my people and my life, but for taking my brother in like this."

Alistaire's gaze followed the young zombie as well. "Trey faces difficult times ahead," *the vampire told her.* "The strength of will that he displayed when he broke free of the heathen priest's control is impressive beyond words, but if he truly wishes to resist his evil nature, as have Sean and I, then he must learn to resist the cannibalistic hunger that will surface within him in a few days." *He afforded himself another small, if sardonic, smile.* "If his hunger matches my thirst, then he already has my sympathy ..."

Gayle trembled and fought against the images that threatened to sweep through her mind, both of the German's plight and her brother's.

Alistaire turned to face her. "I do not speak these morbid, haunting words to unsettle you, Ms. Matthews. I simply want you to know that there are no guarantees that this struggle will succeed. As I said, Trey faces hard times ahead. But ... for what it is worth to you, I believe that he *will* succeed, and that his determination and conviction will soon grant him his wish, to aid Sean and I in our quest."

Gayle nodded. "*Again, thank you, Mr. Bachman. I ... I look forward to seeing you again." She offered him her hand.*

For the first time since they had met, Alistaire was clearly caught off-guard. He then smiled with warmth that almost matched Sean's and accepted her hand, and she was proud to know that she had touched this centuries-old crusader.

"Until next time then," *he said.*

"*Until next time," she agreed.*

Alistaire released her hand, nodded, and headed for the jet.

ELEVEN

After only three weeks of rehearsal, *Deathtrap* opened to a small but very responsive audience. After the opening show, the entire cast, crew, and assorted dates and friends gathered for the cast party at Jimmy Edwards' house, the actor who played Milgrim, the lawyer.

The party started a little after eleven that night. The Edwards' home was nice, and the area was out toward the south side of Norman, so the neighbors were a little more spread out. While there was hardly a fashion code at such an event, I decided to dress for the occasion anyway. Once I'd washed the fake blood off and removed my make-up, I abandoned my usual jeans-and-T-shirt look and instead wore black slacks and shoes and a gold-colored silk shirt. This was a bit out of character for me, and people took note — I even received a few cat-calls!

The party quickly got under full swing. Music played, and a few people danced about the middle of the living room, but most of us ended up standing around gabbing about that night's performance and whatnot. Midnight came and went and the party continued. When one o'clock leered on the horizon, a few people here and there were leaving, and things slowed down a bit. The music was turned down and business had settled almost exclusively into discussion groups of one topic or another. If there's one thing to be said about theatre people, they sure love to talk — amateur philosophers, every one!

I was just opening another wine cooler when my ears pricked up at a conversation between Mike, Jimmy, and Chris Barnes, our Sidney Bruhl of the show.

"Oh, bull*shit*," Jimmy grumbled distastefully. "Don't insult my intelligence. That shit isn't real."

"Hey, I'm tellin' you," Chris returned insistently. "I was one of his examples, and I'm telling you *something* was definitely happening."

"All in your head," Jimmy stated.

"You're being close-minded, Jim," Mike scolded.

"Thank you, Mike," Chris said with a grin.

"Ah-ah-ah! I'm not saying I necessarily believe in it either, I'm just open to the *possibility* that it's real."

"Hey!" I said as I walked over. "What are you guys talking about?"

Jimmy answered, "Chris here took Psychology last semester. He says they taught a few classes on hypnosis, and he's trying to tell us that bullshit is *real*."

"It *is* real, you asshole," Chris insisted.

"Yep," I agreed, "it certainly is." All three turned to me as I grinned broadly. "Sorry, Jimmy, but hypnosis is *very* real."

Chris pointed his finger in Jimmy's face, yelled, "Ha!" and did a little dance.

"Shut up!" Jimmy snapped. He turned back to me. "Are you yankin' my chain?"

"Nope. In fact, I've dabbled in a little of it on my own." *Now* I had them!

"Really?" Kathy asked as she joined us with her brother, Peter, in tow, her interest clearly raised.

"No shit?" Chris asked.

"No shit," I answered.

Several more people began paying attention to the conversation, and I was enjoying every minute of it.

"You're honestly telling me that you've hypnotized people?" Jimmy smirked.

"And been hypnotized several times, yes."

"Interesting," Mike commented.

Chris laughed at Jimmy some more.

Then Kathy suddenly asked, "Do you think you could hypnotize someone here tonight?"

"Yeah," Chris said. "That'll shut Jimmy up."

"Kiss my ass," Jimmy told him. "I'm not believing it until I see it for myself. In fact, I volunteer."

"I wouldn't mind seeing it myself."

"Come on, show them, Neil."

"I'm not buying it, man."

Almost everyone in the room was listening at this point, and my excitement built. Now was my moment!

"Actually, Chris," I said, "I assume you remember what Professor Kullich did to you."

"Yeah, almost every detail."

"I thought you were supposed to go to *sleep*," Jimmy pointed out.

"That's a common misconception," I told him. "Jimmy, do you trust me?"

He blinked. "Well, yeah. Neil, I don't mean that I think you're *lying* to me—"

"I know. What I'm asking is, would you trust me not to ... fake you out, pretend to be hypnotized when I really wasn't?"

"I guess so."

"Yes or no, Jimmy."

He shrugged. "Yes, I trust you."

"Good. In that case, I've got quite a show for you." I sighed and rolled my shoulders and neck. "Chris, I'm going to explain a few things to you first, and then you're going to hypnotize me."

"Why not just hypnotize *me*?" Jimmy demanded.

"I've got a little something I've been working on. If you'll give me a chance, I'll blow you away." I winked at them, and Kathy laughed. "All right, Chris, let's step into the kitchen for a moment."

Taking him aside, I explained what I needed him to do. He felt a little insecure about doing it, concerned that he wouldn't get it right, but I assured him that I was experienced enough to carry the burden and make it work. I needed him as a basic guide, which is all the hypnotizer really is, anyway. I would do the rest. Returning to the living room, I found that I had everyone's undivided attention.

"Jimmy, Mike, could you move this chair so that we have more empty floor to work with, please?"

As they rearranged the Edwards' living room, I addressed my audience, giving them a brief rundown on *The Triumvirate* and the hypnotic games that Mark and I had been playing to develop it.

"Are you serious?" Jimmy asked.

"Very," I answered, "as I'm about to show you. If you'll please turn off all the lights except that lamp, and allow Chris and I about fifteen minutes of absolute quiet, I'll introduce you to a five-and-a-half century old vampire named Alistaire Bachman."

I'd never presented Alistaire with such melodramatic flair, but they seemed riveted. This was even better than the night we showed Lora and Alicia ...

As Alicia passed through my thoughts, I experienced a momentary burst of anxiety. Nothing I could put a name to, just a nagging dread in the back of my mind. Then it passed, and I sat on the floor and continued.

"There are a few things you should know about

Alistaire. He isn't your typical vampire character. In his entire existence as one of the undead, he's never taken a human victim."

"Wait," Kathy interjected. "If he's never bitten anyone, then how does he survive?"

"I said he's never taken a victim," I reminded her. "I didn't say he's never consumed human blood. Alistaire is dedicated to destroying other vampires. That's what the Triumvirate is all about. He's extremely religious and absolutely deplores them."

"A religious vampire?" asked Chris. "How does *that* work?"

"You'll just have to ask Alistaire about that yourself," I told him. Lying back on the carpet with Chris sitting over my head, I added, "Above all else, I want you all to remember that I am in full control of what is about to happen. Inside, I know perfectly well who I really am. In a sense, you can think of this as a higher form of *acting*, an intense performance. I know who I am — the hypnosis merely allows me to put that knowledge in the back of my mind."

With that, I closed my eyes, and at Chris' command, began counting down from one hundred ...

At first awareness, Alistaire felt a wave of disorientation. Even with his eyes closed, he knew that he was surrounded by a group of people, the largest he'd encountered since his voyages into my body. Slowly, he opened his eyes.

Chris looked down at him, his gaze uncertain. "Neil?"

Alistaire shook his head gently from side-to-side.

"Alistaire?"

"Yes."

Alistaire noticed Chris flinch at the change in my voice, and he heard someone else shift uncomfortably. He attempted to sit up, but his balance reeled and he settled back.

"Are you all right?" Chris asked hurriedly.

Alistaire looked at him, but said nothing.

Chris swallowed and said, "My name's Chris Barnes. I'm a friend of Neil's."

Alistaire nodded. *"Where is Mark Hudson?"*

"Um, sorry, I don't know. Are you okay?"

This time Alistaire told him, *"I feel a bit languid. I will be fine in a moment."* He forced himself to sit up and view his surroundings.

As his senses had informed him, the room was filled with nearly twenty young people. Mark was not present, nor was Alex Monroe. The people here were clearly enthralled by his mere presence.

"Alistaire," Chris said from behind him, "I'd like to introduce you to a few people ..."

The young people took turns saying their names. Alistaire followed their voices around to commit the faces to memory as well, but his interest at this point was minimal. He had been in his study reading when the call had come this time.

"Alistaire," Chris said, "would you mind if we ask you a few questions?"

Alistaire sighed inwardly. *Always an interrogation*, he thought. He stepped toward a chair off to one side of the room, seated himself and announced, *"Ask away."*

"Alistaire?" a young lady said.

He regarded her. It was the attractive girl with the German last name. *"Katherine, isn't it?"*

She smiled. "Yes. I just wanted you to know that ... well, I don't want you to feel that you're on the spot here. I mean, Neil didn't bring you here just as a guinea pig. I could tell in his voice that he was proud of you, likes you. We'd just like a chance to get to know you ourselves."

That brought a few raised eyebrows and exchanged glances from the rest of the group. I myself, from my adjacent viewpoint, felt a bit taken aback from her statement. After all, I *had*, in fact, brought Alistaire here to show him off. The impact of the pronouncement was not lost on Alistaire.

"Why, thank you, Ms. Schaumburg," he said. *"I'll keep that in mind."*

Kathy smiled.

With a new attitude toward the evening, Alistaire said, *"Who is first?"*

The initial questions were understandably predictable and too repetitive to record here — these people had never met Alistaire. They wanted to know where he was from, what he did, how he fed himself, when he did this, how he did that, the same questions Mark and Alex asked in the beginning. Alistaire answered them politely, and with steadily increasing interest. He found that these young people were indeed amicable and bright, especially Kathy. The evening was turning out much better than he first expected — he even approved of what I was wearing for the first time!

A few question *did* come up that I hadn't heard before. Someone — Mike, I believe — asked him about the toughest battle he'd ever fought, but Alistaire barely mentioned something called "the Brigade" before he was interrupted by someone spilling a beer on the carpet. At another point, Chris raised his hand and, when pointed to, asked, "Alistaire, what denomination are you?"

"Religious denomination?"

"Yes."

"I am a Chris—tian."

Chris wasn't satisfied. "Yeah, but what *specific* faith do you follow? I'm Baptist myself. I don't remember off the top of my head when the Protestant church spread out. Was Germany under Catholic influence at that time, or ..."

Alistaire gestured for him to stop. *"I do not believe in petty squabbles over church politics. I believe in G-God. I accept Chr-Christ as my Savior. That is all. I have read the Bible for myself, and I follow the path which It spoke to my heart. Personally, I feel that the Catholics have placed their Pope far too close to He-Heaven, and I find their considerable earthly, material wealth more than a little hypocritical. Then again, I mean no offense, but I also find foolish notions held by some Protestant denominations, such as the popular insistence that* dancing *is somehow sinful, quite laughable. As far as I am concerned, if you believe in G-God and Chr-Christ, and follow His word of having no other G-God before Him, and loving thy brother as thyself, then politics should not matter. Ch-Christ is above such things."*

Chris mused over what Alistaire had said. I silently thanked him for posing an issue that I'd never before heard Alistaire address. I myself was raised Episcopalian and had never consciously thought about it in that light.

"Alistaire?" Kathy asked quietly. He looked her way. "I notice whenever you mention God or Christ, you sort of stutter. Is it painful for you to say those Names?"

"Only in my throat, Ms. Schaumburg, not in my heart."

"Alistaire," Peter, Kathy's brother, asked suddenly, his first words since the vampire's arrival, "you said that you're from Germany, so you speak German, of course?"

"Of course," Alistaire answered after a moment's hesitation. *"Unfortunately, I've found that—"*

"Dann verstehst du mich," Peter continued.

Well, Alistaire thought, *this is much more pleasant.* He answered, *"Ich verstehe Sie sehr gut, danke. Sie kennen doch Ihre Familienchronik?"*

Peter grumbled ambiguously. Kathy stared at him. "Why did you ask him that?"

"Ask him what?" piped in Chris. "What was that all about?"

"Mr. Schaumburg was simply confirming that I had not lied to him about my linguistic skills."

Peter remained silent, and it seemed to Alistaire that he was fuming. How odd. He might have pressed the matter, but at that point Jimmy announced, to the many groans and jibes of the crowd around him, that it was getting late and he needed to close things down. "But, Alistaire," he added, "be sure to let Neil know that he's made a believer out of me."

"You may tell him yourself, Jim. If you have decided to retire, it is probably best if I return home as well."

No one seemed too happy about it, but no one protested, either. The general audience broke up then, leaving only Kathy, Peter, Jimmy, and Mike to watch as Chris prepared Alistaire for departure.

"It's been really nice meeting you, Alistaire," Kathy said as he rested prone on the floor.

"The feeling is mutual, Katherine, I assure you." Then he added, *"The same to all of you, of course."*

"Listen," she continued, "I'm sure we'll be getting together several more times before the semester is over. Will you promise to drop by again?"

Alistaire regarded her. It was almost as if ... but no, who did he think he was, Sean Mallory? *"Consider it a promise. And now, Christopher, if you will ..."*

Chris waved his verbal wand, and within three minutes I was back and discussing the event with everyone. I was quite pleased with how things had gone. Everyone expressed interest in seeing Alistaire again.

Maybe it was the rush of sharing Alistaire once more. Maybe it was the company of friends, the still-lingering thrill of *Deathtrap's* success, or the new way I was beginning to look at Kathy. Or maybe it was a little impediment placed by Alistaire Bachman.

Whatever the answer, it somehow never dawned on me to question the fact that I do not, nor have I ever, spoken a single word of German.

XII

1748. London. Night.

Catherine the harlot sighed openly as the local clock struck three. She had been working the streets since sundown, and not a single taker. It did not help her disposition that this had been typical of the past week, and not much different from the two weeks preceding that. Perhaps she was simply getting too old and unattractive for the profession. She didn't want to believe it, of course, but the other women in the area didn't seem to be having any undo trouble of late. The question was moot, since no matter how she felt about herself these days, she still needed to put bread on the table for herself and her daughter, and if that meant staying out later than she preferred, then so be it.

Leaning against the alley corner which served as her "breezy disappearance" route if a bobby happened to wander by, she shifted her weight onto one leg, then the other in a futile search for relief for her aching feet. No such comfort appeared forthcoming, but what else did she have to do at the moment?

A footstep to her left roused her attention, and she casually turned her head to steal a glance. She nearly screamed when she found the owner standing barely three feet from her.

"Oh!" she exclaimed, placing her hand over her heart. "You nearly scared the life out of me, sir!"

"My apologies, madame," *the man responded in a silky voice.*

Catherine examined her unannounced visitor from head to toe. The man was richly dressed, though not in an excessively tasteful *fashion, but she knew all too well that beggars could not afford to be choosers. The man held his hat in hand, and she could see by the light of the nearby lantern that he was fairly handsome, if a little on the pale side. Still, his fair skin complimented his porcelain-smooth complexion, and she finally rated him as an above-average customer.*

Of course, he had yet to actually breach the subject.

"Taking a late night walk, are we, sir?" she asked coyly, pulling her shoulders back just enough to subtly thrust her breasts forward.

"Indeed, madame," *the man replied with a hint of a smile,* "I do sincerely hope that we are both aware of why I approached you." *He reached out with his free hand and gently brushed the knuckles across the swell of her bosom.*

Catherine pursed her lips. At least his straight-forward manner would save time and get her home that much earlier.

"In that case, sir," she purred in her softer, sultry voice, "where would you like to do our business?"

The man looked up and down the deserted street, then glanced over her shoulder into the alleyway. He smiled, took her hand, and pulled her in that direction, quickly steering them into the shadows.

"Sir!" Catherine protested as she struggled to keep with his brisk pace. He gave no acknowledgment as he led them deep into the darkness. Well, he was not her first customer who wished to take her outside on the very streets,

and she knew that he probably would not be her last.

Finally, as they neared the back wall with the only light shining from a lantern poised in a window high above, the man stopped and turned to her. He now gazed at her with such open hunger that she found herself momentarily unsettled.

"Er, sir," she said, reminding herself firmly that business was business, "not to temper your mood, but I do wish to discuss payment before we begin."

The man laughed, and it was a frosty, callous laughter that chilled Catherine to the bone.

*"Payment?" the man cackled. "*I do not give payment for what I want when I have but to *take* it!"

Catherine gaped in horror, a scream lodging somewhere in the back of her throat, as the man opened his mouth to reveal hideous, wolf-like fangs. His eyes shimmered and shifted from deep brown to an electric, glowing blue. His jaw elongated, giving him a maw that matched the nature of his canines. His fingers stretched in similar fashion, growing into sharp talons. His lips, distorted as they were, twisted into a wicked smile as he reached for her throat.

Catherine had yet to find her voice when the need to scream came into sudden, unexpected question. A fraction of a second before the man-monster's claws touched her skin, a shape moving so swiftly it was nothing but a blur flew past her, the rush of its wake blowing her physically back against the alley wall. It smashed into her attacker with thunderous force. The shape knocked the man-monster from his feet, sending him crashing into a large pile of garbage.

A few wondrous blinks from Catherine revealed the shape to be yet another man-monster, this one appearing marginally more human than the first. He wore a gentleman's clothing of much richer material and design than her attacker's. The newcomer's wavy, black hair swept away from his face to reveal similar large fangs, although his mouth and jaw retained human proportions. His eyes burned, not blue, but solid white. His hands also held ordinary shape, though Catherine found the fingernails noticeably longer and sharper than most men wore them. Her instincts demanded that she recoil from this newcomer, but she clearly could not outrun him if he gave chase, so she held her ground. Plus, whoever he was, he had just saved her from her attacker, who, for what more it was worth, was the more ghastly of the two. She clamped her hand over her mouth to stifle her whimper as her assailant threw the trash away from himself.

The first creature rose to his feet, his terrible face warping further with prominent rage. He glanced briefly at Catherine, then addressed her defender, "What the hell are you doing?! Find your own prey! You're lucky I don't report you to the Brigade for this outra—"

With another blitz of inhuman speed, the Defender leaped forward and seized the creature. The beast's astonishment was evident as the Defender slammed him from wall to wall with a strength capable of staggering even a supernatural being. He tried futilely to free himself from the Defender's grasp, and cried out in frustration when his efforts failed.

Catherine watched in awe as her Defender swung the creature back and forth as if he weighed nothing. She was no less impressed, and unnerved, by the creature's durability. The stone itself was beginning to crack, while the numerous blows had yet to draw blood.

Still, the repeated impacts eventually took their toll, and the creature ceased what little resistance he had been able to offer. The Defender threw him to the ground, then *leaned over him. He glanced halfway over his shoulder toward Catherine, mindful not to bring his frightening eyes fully to bear upon her.* "Are you all right, madame?" *he asked in a strange accent that reminded her of a German gentleman she had once serviced.*

"I believe so," she told him in a shaky voice.

The Defender again turned upon the creature. He closed his strong hand upon the dazed creature's throat and pinned him in a kneeling position against the near wall.

"Who are you?" *the creature asked in a tight, spiteful voice.* "What do you want?"

"My name is Alistaire Bachman," *the Defender told him,* "and I want to ask you a few questions."

" 'Alistaire Bachman?' " *the creature repeated. A look of recognition passed over his twisted face.* "I've heard of you. You're the German traitor who hunts his own kind." *The creature managed a quick smile.* "The Brigade has plans for you."

"You have heard of me, and I have heard of this 'Brigade.' In fact, I have journeyed to England to meet them. Unfortunately, I do not know as much about them as I would prefer." *Alistaire, as the Defender had now named himself, leaned forward, staring into his captive's face.* "You will now share with me everything that you know about them."

"Go to hell, jerry!" *the creature spat in contempt.*

Alistaire stared at him intently. "Doubtful," *he said. He then asked,* "What is your name?"

The creature appeared confused by this shift of subject, but answered, "Charles."

"Charles," *Alistaire repeated calmly. He next asked,* "How old are you, Charles?"

Again, the creature answered despite his obvious bewilderment. "One-hundred-seven."

"Mmm. One-hundred-seven. Still a bit on the young side, at least for one of us, eh, Charles?"

Charles tried to sit forward. Alistaire held him where he was.

"You take pleasure from your power, don't you, Charles? Your power to hunt mortals, to take their life's blood at your leisure?" *Alistaire tightened his grip on the younger vampire's throat and leaned forward until their eyes were mere inches apart. His free hand shot forward like a snake and closed over Charles' chest, his clawed fingertips digging inward a fraction of an inch. His eyes shimmered more fiercely even as Charles' appeared to dim.* "You are in a new position now, Charles. *You* are the helpless prey before the predator. And if you do not tell me everything that I want to know, I will end your existence as easily as you would this woman's."

With that, Charles began to panic. He hissed and spat and struggled with an animalistic fury that again filled Catherine with the urge to run, but the mortal woman was now as enthralled by this supernatural drama as she was horrified by it, and she found that she needed to know how it ended.

Charles and Alistaire continued their very one-sided struggle for several seconds. Then, just when it seemed about to end, Catherine met yet another sight that stretched the limits of her comprehension. Charles dissolved before her very eyes, his body melting into some kind of bluish mist. This fog swirled formlessly out of Alistaire's grasp and began to drift up the alley wall when Alistaire also faded into a cloud, his white-grey in hue. The ivory mist swept around and thoroughly blanketed the blue. The blue mist flowed to and fro, like thin liquid in a crystal globe, seeking some escape. There was none to be found. Slowly, the two independent fogs solidified into their respective humanoid shapes, with Alistaire again holding Charles by throat and chest.

"I warn you, Charles," *the German said calmly.* "I will not ask again."

Charles grumbled and slumped in defeat. "If I help you, will you free me?" *Alistaire paused, then issued a curt nod.* "What do you want to know?"

"Tell me about the Brigade. I know they number three, powerful vampires. I know patriotism shapes their unlikely bond. No vampires have ever worked together successfully in the past; their selfish natures tend to undermine most group efforts."

"The Brigade have managed to overcome the 'selfish natures' you refer to," *Charles told him, his voice dripping with sarcasm.* "True, they are three Englishmen. They are building their throngs at a consistent pace, usually from street urchins who will not be easily missed, and they share control of their new minions. They have also contacted many of the preexisting vampires throughout London and the surrounding area. All those who swear loyalty to their cause enjoy regulation of hunting areas, and unity against self-serving rogues like you."

Alistaire smirked. "I doubt that any other 'rogues' you've dealt with have shared my motivations."

Charles shrugged as best he could. "I could not care less about your 'motivations,' as you say. Any vampire, English or not, who attempts to upset the status quo are dealt with by the Brigade. And when the Brigade spread their influence throughout the rest of Europe and the Colonies, and the world, any who refuse to pledge their loyalty and obedience to the Brigade and to England's flag will be destroyed."

Alistaire looked thoughtful at this. "An interesting notion, this patriotism amongst vampires. Such a stronghold could prove virtually invincible against any outside threat, be it of mortal or supernatural origin." *He sighed deeply.* "I must stop them before their efforts take shape."

Charles forced a laugh. "Idiot. *Fool*! It is too late to stop them. The Brigade is a fact! You cannot do anything to stop them!"

"We'll see," *Alistaire said, facing his captive full on.* "Thank you, Charles. You have been most helpful."

Without warning, Alistaire thrust his arm forward, his hand penetrating Charles' chest with surprisingly little effort. Charles hissed, his muscles growing rigid, then relaxing abruptly as Alistaire removed his heart. An expression of peace passed over his face and he fell to the side, his body already crumbling with his age, sixty years of eager, impatient death no longer held at bay.

Catherine lowered her hand, which had been tightly covering her mouth. She regarded Alistaire with apprehension as he stood and rounded toward her.

"You have nothing to fear from me," *he told her. Catherine nodded briefly, then her gaze shot past him to Charles' rapidly decomposing body. Alistaire glanced over his shoulder.* "I told him that if he helped me, I would free him. I have done just that."

Catherine nodded again. Her calm was assisted by the fact that Alistaire Bachman now wore the appearance of a normal, not unattractive man in his early- to mid-thirties. She cleared her throat. "Sir, I could not help but hear you ask that ... that man about the Brigade."

Alistaire eyed her with new interest. "Yes?"

Catherine swallowed and said, "Sir, I know of the Brigade as well. Everyone *knows the Brigade.*"

Alistaire gave her his undivided attention, and although his eyes now appeared human, they still possessed an unnerving strength that caused her gaze to shy away.

"They are well known about London," she continued. *"Rich men, they are. They own a great deal of property and businesses around the city. They are called 'Sirs,' though I can't attest myself whether or not they've actually been knighted or the like. The 'Brigade' is the name of their business association."*

"And what are their individual names?" *he asked.*

"I believe, sir, that their names are Sir Kenton, Sir Lloyd, and Sir Bishop."

Alistaire absorbed this, then asked, "Madame, what is *your* name?"

Catherine actually blushed as she told him.

"Catherine," *Alistaire said as he gently led her away from the carnage behind him,* "could you possibly tell me the names and locations of a few of the Brigade's businesses?"

* * *

Kenton sipped at his drink, savoring the exquisite taste of the crimson liquid swirling within the chalice, then set it upon the elegant marble and glass stand beside his high-backed chair. His tongue lightly brushed at the residual blood upon his lips as he said, "Then let us now call the meeting to order."

Kenton, Lloyd, and Bishop, accompanied only by a single secretary under Kenton's command, thus opened their weekly meeting of the Brigade. They met this time in the study of one of Lloyd's personal estates in a wealthy district outside of London proper. The lush surroundings pleased Bishop's senses as much now as when he'd first joined his fellow British to form their triad. Of the three, Bishop had led his mortal life in the comparatively lowest social standing. While he had not exactly been dirt poor, *his meager childhood home held nothing against any of Lloyd's numerous dwellings. His financial status was far greater now after more than fifty years as a vampire, but he was still third in wealth as well as age under his two associates. Lloyd and Kenton treated him as their equal, but Bishop eagerly anticipated the day when he could personally afford houses as rich and abundant as did Lloyd.*

Bishop listened as the secretary, Elizabeth, a luscious young wench whom Kenton openly shared, issued a reading of the minutes from their previous meeting. He relaxed in a fancy settee opposite Kenton's chair before the large, stone fireplace. Lloyd sat behind his oak desk, with Elizabeth reading from a lower chair on his left. The leaping, shadowy light of the flames cast flickering illumination across the high bookshelves, stained glass windows, and expensive, gold candelabras. Many elitists found silver a more appealing casing for their hand-designed candles, but Lloyd's desire to keep that metal out of his home called no inquiries from his fellow Brigade.

"Elizabeth," *Kenton ordered in his nonchalant fashion,* "note that our first order of business tonight is the expansion of our influence across the channel into France."

"Yes,   Sir   Kenton,"   Elizabeth   acknowledged submissively.

Bishop smiled privately at her hush, mortal-like tone. Kenton liked to keep his harem under a tight leash.

"Sir Lloyd," *Kenton continued,* "have your preliminary queries gone well?"

"They have," *Lloyd answered.* "I have established promising lines of communication with half a dozen of our kind in the city of Paris. Four of them have expressed strong interest in following our reign. The other two are more than willing to consider any formal proposition we have to make."

"Very good," *Kenton pronounced with a slight nod.* "If things continue as planned, we should be prepared to make our move within the year."

"I personally look forward to a subtle conquest of the French," *Bishop said with a mischievous grin.* "Perhaps after a century or two, we might even improve upon their manners."

The three men and Elizabeth shared a hearty laugh at the jest. They were, after all, British to the bone.

As their laughter faded, Lloyd cleared his throat and said, "There was one note of interest that I feel I should mention. I believe we have discussed both officially and off-the-record the scourge named Bachman from Germany."

The atmosphere darkened considerably. Bishop nodded, while Kenton acknowledged the statement with a deep-throated grunt.

"On the necessary assumption that the rumors are true, I have attempted to track any known movements from Bachman outside his country. While Bachman himself has proven elusive, the slaughter of our kind, particularly when no mortal hunters appear to be involved, inevitably causes ripples."

Kenton again grunted, deeper this time. Bishop also noticed increasing agitation from Elizabeth.

"While seeking out the elder vampires of Paris, my servants happened upon some rather disturbing news spreading through France. It seems ..."

Lloyd's voice trailed off as he noticed the change in Kenton's expression, which shifted swiftly from abstract anger to a more immediate alertness and intensity. Bishop glanced over to see what had given Lloyd such pause, and he, too, felt confusion and a trace of foreboding at the elder vampire's abrupt change in disposition.

Suddenly, Kenton leaped to his feet, his fangs bared

and his eyes awash with a crimson glow. "Lloyd! Behind you!"

The barest fraction of an instant before Kenton's warning, Bishop also spotted the invader. Any true vampire could recognize another's metaform for what it was. The column of mist erupting from the tiny crevice in the wall descended upon Lloyd before either of his colleagues could respond.

Lloyd was far from a fledgling, and to his credit he made a valiant effort to resist, but much to his misfortune, he himself was not a mist-vampire. *Shape-shifting into his bat metaform would have proven little help, so he tried instead to leap over his desk to escape his attacker. He might have made it but for the invader's impressive speed. Drawing into humanoid form, the invader seized Lloyd around the throat, one clawed hand digging into his flesh from the front, the other from the back. Lloyd had time for a single cry of indignation and fear before the other vampire ripped his head from his body.*

This impossible sight stunned Bishop and even Kenton into immobility. Elizabeth scrambled away from the man, screaming senselessly until Kenton silenced her with an angry mental command. The idea, the mere notion *that a leader of the Brigade could so quickly and easily fall prey to another vampire was too ridiculous to even consider ... yet they had just witnessed that very act.*

The invader casually tossed Lloyd's head onto his desk. The body stood for a moment longer before falling to the side. Completely composed, the man spoke, "The Brigade, I presume." *He bowed with his head.*

Kenton's upper lip curled in cold fury as he recognized the German touch to the man's words. "Bachman!"

Alistaire again bowed from the neck.

Bishop was dumbstruck. Not more than a minute

earlier they had been contemptuously discussing the German rogue, and now he stood before them with Lloyd destroyed at his feet. It was not possible. The Brigade was invincible!

The pool of ichor beneath Lloyd's head slowly spread across the desk.

Kenton spoke again, his voice more controlled but no less icy. "I must admit, despite myself, that I am impressed, Bachman — moving through the house while escaping our notice, *my* notice. I did not even sense you until ..." *His crimson eyes dropped to glance at Lloyd's head, then lifted to again lock with Alistaire's.* "... until it was too late. And let us not forget to mention that Sir Lloyd was a vampire of more than two hundred years."

Bishop scrutinized their opponent carefully. An aura of power surrounding him that unnerved the relatively young vampire. Bishop was unusually strong for his age, with a will that had benefitted him greatly since his transition into his undead state. Many new vampires who were products of random feeding frenzies, as was Bishop's case, left without a known master or guide, found themselves severely disoriented through their early years, often falling victim to any number of destructive fates before finding their focus. Bishop, on the other hand, managed to pull himself together in less than a week, slipping into his new pattern of existence with the ease of one a century his elder.

Still, Bishop would have been deeply apprehensive over a confrontation with a vampire Lloyd's age. And Bachman had dispatched Lloyd effortlessly.

"I seek neither your praise nor your admiration," *Alistaire said. He moved around the desk, causing Elizabeth to again whimper and cower at Kenton's side.* "I will not allow you to spread your corruption to France or anywhere else. I have come to destroy you."

"How *noble* of you," *Kenton smirked.* "Pathetic *kraut*! What respect you gain by ability you lose by despicable disposition." *He glanced first at Bishop, then Elizabeth.* "We have nothing to fear from this oaf." *He then smiled openly at Alistaire.* "You have overstepped yourself this time, Bachman. Now that you have exposed yourself, I see you for what you are." *He paused, his self-confidence brimming to new limits.* "How old are you, Bachman? Two centuries? Three?"

Alistaire said nothing. Kenton straightened to his full height, his scarlet eyes glistening in the firelight.

"I have existed for over half a *millennium*, kraut. I have faced many challenges and crises and have always persevered. You have plagued our kind far too long already."

He looked to Elizabeth. She drew back in terror.

"Do not question me, woman!" *he bellowed.*

Elizabeth bowed her head, turned, and leaped at Alistaire.

The German vampire did not even blink. He blocked her assault, ripped open her chest, and pulled out her heart. She stared at it without comprehension before collapsing. Alistaire dropped it beside Lloyd's withering head.

"Little bother," *Kenton commented idly.* "I had grown tired of her recently. As you are about to learn, jerry, Sir Bishop and I will not be so easily defeated."

*   *   *

Alistaire Bachman had never battled so hard.

Lloyd's large study lay in shambles. The three struggling vampires had carried the battle through the southern wall and into the great living room.

The heart of the fight belonged to Alistaire and Kenton, with Bishop offering his fellow Brit whatever assistance he could. All three sported multiple claw and teeth wounds, their clothing hanging in tatters. At one point, Kenton and the German had fought the battle in their mist forms, leaving Bishop, who was a bat-vampire like Lloyd, with little to do except send mental commands to the vampires in the area he had created. Lloyd had always enjoyed the privacy of their meetings, and it would take some time before any help could arrive.

With a wail of satisfaction, Kenton whirled and threw Alistaire the length of the living room. The German vampire slammed into the stone mantle over this room's hearth, then fell in a stunned heap before the fire. Although this presented the Englishmen with an excellent opportunity to burn him, they instead strode slowly and smugly after him. The remaining Brigade leaders were now confident that their nemesis' time was limited, and they chose to enjoy their revenge exacted in Lloyd's name.

"Not feeling so saucy now, are you, kraut?" *Kenton laughed.*

Bishop joined him. How had he ever feared this Alistaire Bachman? Granted, he would dread fighting him alone, but the jerry obviously had no chance against Sir Kenton, much less the two of them together. Sir Lloyd's loss would be greatly felt — despite the vicious nature of vampires, he was indeed their friend as well as business partner. But the Brigade would recover, and prosper, and there was nothing Alistaire Bachman could do about it.

Alistaire rose shakily to his hands and knees. It had been centuries since he had felt the wind knocked out of him. It never occurred to him that it was still possible, or that it would matter *if it happened — perhaps vampires needed to breathe more than they liked to think. He absently noted the fact as a possible explanation for why some vampires who hibernated never awoke ...*

Enough! Urgent, deadly business was at hand! Idle speculation about trivial facts could wait their turn.

Alistaire now realized that he had grown brash in recent years. After his second century, it seemed that almost all the vampires he exterminated were younger than he, often significantly so. Occasionally he encountered one close to his age, as he just had in eastern France, but he had never before fought an opponent with so much time over him as Sir Kenton, not even Mikhail. If he wished to survive and continue his crusade, he must act soon.

As he listened to Kenton and Bishop's leisurely approach, he noticed that his tremendous impact had caused more damage to the fireplace than the naked eye could see. The hearth shifted noticeably beneath him as he moved. The house must have a basement, perhaps a wine cellar, for he could tell that he was not over solid earth. If he were cunning, he could use this deduction to help even the odds.

Lifting his head, he saw that the two Englishmen were spreading to outflank him.

Good.

Turning to look at Bishop, Alistaire smiled broadly to the verge of laughter.

Bishop blinked. "I see precious little for you to be smiling about, kraut."

Hoping it sounded convincing, Alistaire forced a chuckle. "I appear to have more reason than *you*, my bigoted friend. Even if I am destroyed here and now, at least I leave this world as my own person, rather than a hapless minion."

A moment passed before Bishop released his own smile. "You know little of the Brigade. We formed our group for mutual benefit. Sir Kenton is my partner, not my master."

"I'm sure it pleases him for you to believe that, but as my exposure has allowed him to inspect me, my proximity has also allowed me to examine the two of you. You are the product of an indiscriminate feeding attack, are you not, Mr. Bishop?"

Bishop's face slackened. Alistaire thanked the Lord for his lucky guess.

Kenton's eyes narrowed during the exchange. Only his bold assurance that Alistaire was now harmless kept his approach slow. "Aimless stalling will not help you, Bachman," *the elder vampire proclaimed.*

Alistaire ignored him, keeping his attention on Bishop. "A vampire your age cannot sense what we can," *Alistaire told him.* "A link exists between master and slave, Mr. Bishop, a tangible bond. Your manner of creation left you in a void, with neither a master nor self-achieved independence. It is now obvious that Kenton has stepped into your void."

For a brief moment, Bishop's eyes darted toward Kenton.

"Don't be gullible, Sir Bishop," *Kenton snapped with vast indignation and perhaps a touch of genuine hurt in his voice.* "Have I ever commanded you to do anything against your will? Does your mind cloud in my presence? You have slaves of your own — you know how total the domination of will is. Are you in any way similar to them?"

"Over 'half a millennium,' he claims," *Alistaire hammered.* "More than sufficient time to perfect his methods of control. Perhaps even conceal them?"

Bishop's confusion grew, giving way to anger. He had ceased his approach and trembled in tense bewilderment.

"Bishop, look at me!" *Kenton raged. Bishop obeyed.* "I am an Englishman! I am also your friend. I give you my word as a gentlemen and a patriot, this jerry is lying to divide us and save himself!"

Bishop's gaze returned to Alistaire. The German smiled and shook his head in pity. "Puppet."

"Liar!" *Bishop screamed as he charged his enemy.*

"Bishop, *wait!" Kenton cried, but his warning fell on deaf ears.*

The British and German vampires collided, and Alistaire added his own strength to Bishop's momentum when they slammed against the hearth. The stone cracked, then split. The floor surrounding the hearth buckled slightly. Holding Bishop at bay with one hand, Alistaire planted his heels and heaved his back against the fireplace. The flames licked at his right shoulder, but he ignored the pain as he pushed with all of his supernatural might.

A hiss from his left — fangs bared and claws extended, Kenton leaped. Alistaire's heart sank.

His crusade was over.

The barest instant before Kenton reached them, the entire hearth tilted and the floor divided. A gaping cavity materialized and swallowed the hearth, Alistaire, and Bishop. They crashed onto the floor of the cellar, the vampires twisting to face each other. Then, with a crashing roar, the entire fireplace, stone casing, burning embers and all, descended toward them. Alistaire leaped away. Bishop was not so lucky. The blazing inferno consumed him, and he was gone from sight.

"Bishop!" *Kenton called from above. Despite his enhanced senses, he could not see anything but the flames. Nor could he hear Bishop, or Bachman. Regardless of the dictates of caution, he would have to leap down to the cellar. The fire was spreading and time was limited, but he could not leave without knowing the fates of both his ally and his enemy.*

So intent was he on the sight below, he failed to notice

the ivory mist rising within the ebony smoke. He sensed danger the moment before Alistaire reformed and seized him from behind. The German leaped upon Kenton and locked his legs around his chest, pinning his arms.

"I am afraid you will not live to see your next quincentennial, Mr. Kenton."

Kenton did not decapitate as easily as Lloyd, however, and before it was over he had bitten through Alistaire's left forearm to the bone. He almost escaped as he tried shifting into his mist form. If Alistaire had not had both arms, both legs, and his back into the effort, his leverage would not have been enough.

When it was over and Kenton's head was tossed into the rising flames, Alistaire turned to leave and nearly collapsed. Only a nearby chair saved him from falling to his knees. The loss of blood sapped his strength and gave rise to his hunger. He would have to at least hunt some cat or dog before sunrise, and visit a hospital or morgue before departing for home. His wounds would take several nights to heal. Maybe this was a sign that it was time to relocate and renew his hunt upon fresh grounds. He would miss Germany dearly, but he must obey his Divine calling.

His senses told him that other vampires were coming. Young though they were, he was in no shape to meet them. Dissolving into mist, Alistaire stole away into the night.

* * *

Bishop's thralls arrived minutes later, just in time to see the first tongues of fire lash through the windows. The seven vampires, each less than a decade as undead, ambled about in indecision. The forceful presence of the Brigade was missing from the house. The threat Bishop's call had warned of had obviously gotten the best of them.

A shriek of rage and pain chilled their already cold blood, and one of the low cellar windows exploded outward as a humanoid bat emerged. Fire seared the vampire's clothing and wings, and the thralls hurried to extinguish the blaze. It was a man-bat that hit the ground, but it was Sir Bishop whom the minions rolled onto his back.

"Help me home," *he commanded.* "Then bring me something to drink."

His servants obeyed, carrying him away in the opposite direction that Alistaire had taken.

The night was frosty, but Bishop's burns made it feel decidedly warm. His burns, and his blistering hatred — a rancor that would not soon fade.

THIRTEEN

Another week slipped away as Mark and I continued to research our characters. I'd finished the plot for the premiere issue, and Mark had penciled about half of it. The process moved a little slower than would be allowed if we actually succeeded in publishing it as a monthly title, but Mark really wanted the first issue to shine, to win the editors' interests. I was more than happy to allow my ideas for the next issue to marinate.

The same week witnessed other points of interest. While Alicia and I were apparently destined for no more of each other, Mark and Lora now saw each other constantly. Or rather, *Sean* and Lora did. It seemed the hot-and-horny young dancer couldn't get enough of the equally-horny, older Irishman, even if he did occupy the body of Mark Hudson.

Mark ...

My schedule was hectic — in addition to my classes and work on the comic, an extra weekend had been added to *Deathtrap's* original run — but I would have been blind not to notice the changes in him. He had skipped more classes in the past month than he had in his entire previous years of college. His smoking habit had dropped to almost nothing, but any money he might have saved was instead spent on beer and any Irish drinks he could find. Sean Mallory could certainly handle these quantities with ease, but I feared for Mark's constitution, and his bank account. He was also plagued by perpetual headaches. I suspected they originated from the time Sean spent with Lora, which left Mark without his glasses for long periods, but unfortunately Mark insisted that he could see just fine while doing Sean and would hear nothing of it.

"Could Mark be addicted to hypnosis?" Alex asked me at one point, and I wasn't sure how to answer him. My strict knowledge of hypnosis insisted that it wasn't possible — my gut was starting to tell me otherwise. Basically, Mark was still Mark. He wasn't exhibiting the signs of a total breakdown like a stereotypical addict. Because of this, I didn't put my foot down, and our characterization experiments continued.

As things progressed, we realized that while Alistaire often talked about Sean and vice versa, we had never taken the opportunity to see them *together*. Mark insisted we rectify that oversight.

Flipping through the pages of my new hypnosis book, a little paperback I had taken to carrying with me everywhere I went, Alex assured us that he had watched us enough times that he could manage to get us both down — after Chris' success at the *Deathtrap* party, I felt confident he was right. Together he and I sketched out the guidelines for a fill-in-the-blank process, in which neither Alistaire nor Sean would be mentioned by name. Mark and I would slip our appropriate characters in on our own, allowing us to listen and use Alex's voice simultaneously. We also left room for Alex to improvise so that we couldn't anticipate his every word.

We met at Alex's apartment for a change — Mark brought along his sketch book, of course, to show me the pages he had finished for the premiere issue and his latest werewolf illustrations. After the sun set, we cleared the living room floor so that Mark and I could lie comfortably head-to-head. We slowed our breathing and closed our eyes as Alex killed the overhead light.

"Deep relaxing breaths ..." he began.

Even before his eyes opened, Alistaire caught the one scent that he simply could not miss — a scent that reminded him vaguely of a wet dog.

With a warm smile, Alistaire sat up and glanced over his shoulder. *"Hello, Sean."*

"Alistaire," the Irishman returned. He rocked back, then forward into a crouch, twisting around at the same time to face his German friend. "Bit different seein' ye like this."

"And you as well." Alistaire looked to Alex. *"Hello again."*

"Hi," Alex returned with a short wave.

"Leave you alone with us tonight, did they?" Sean chided.

"I'm afraid so."

"No problem. We felt your call and I made sure to explain to Trey that he wasn't to go anywhere until we get back."

Alex nodded. In an earlier session, Sean had explained that when we called him or Alistaire, they actually had to *leave* wherever it was that they "came from," which was, to their perception, the townhouse in Pittsburgh.

Alistaire rose to his feet now and moved about the sparse apartment. He noted that the previous tenant had been a smoker. Alex obviously was not. He also noticed that Mark's body reeked of it less and less.

Sean had also begun to look around, and he called to Alistaire from the hallway leading to the bathroom and bedroom. The vampire stepped around the corner to join his comrade ...

... and stopped dead in his tracks.

Sean stood grinning before the full length mirror hanging from the hall closet door. His back was to his friend and he used the reflection to wink. Seeing Sean's reflection was one thing, but Alistaire was totally unprepared to cast one of his own.

For *my* part, I saw only myself. As Alistaire walked slowly to the glass in stunned amazement, his bewilderment was so overwhelming that I could not tell for certain exactly what he was viewing.

My question was echoed by Sean. "What do ye see in there?"

"I ... I see Neil," Alistaire answered. *"What do* you *see?"*

"I see Mark, but I also see myself a bit. It's hard to describe."

"I reflect only Neil, which I suppose makes sense in my case. But still ..." He reached out to gently touch the mirror. *"... I am not used to reflecting anything at all."*

Alex, who had stepped into the hallway to stand behind them, asked, "Why *is* that, by the way? Do you have any idea why vampires don't cast reflections?"

Still enamored by my image, Alistaire paused a few moments before responding. In that brief time, I felt a surprisingly strong wave of emotion wash through him. The experience was ... remarkable. Until now, the strongest emotions I'd felt through him were his fear the night of Mikhail's attack, and his undying devotion to God and to his cause. What I felt now was a deep, mournful *need*, a longing so intense it was difficult not to get swept away by it. A longing to be mortal again, to be human.

As quickly as it struck, the sentiment passed. Alistaire instantly composed himself. *"I am afraid I do not know for certain. I have asked that question myself a few times but have found no answers. I do have a theory, for what it is worth."*

"Please, share it," Alex urged.

Alistaire collected his thoughts and said, *"Essentially, it boils down to our undead state. Simply put: We should not be here. Granted, we have more physical substance than that of a ghost, but the fact remains that I died over five centuries ago.* I should no longer exist in this world. *It has been said that photographs and mirrors capture and reflect one's immortal soul. As I believe vampires to be soulless creatures, I find it fitting that our image cannot be grasped by either medium. I admit it is also discomforting as I, too, am a vampire, but it is not my place to question G-God's will."*

"Enough o' this deep, dark discussion," Sean interjected suddenly — he seemed more unsettled by this line of reasoning than Alistaire. "Alex, do ye have anything to eat here, lad?"

"Oh, uh, no, not really. I've been needing to go to the grocery store for a while."

"Damn," Sean sighed. "I'm hungry."

"Actually," Alistaire said as the thought donned on him, *"I am as well. At least, Neil is. It has been a long time since I have felt this sort of hunger."* He glanced at my reflection once more. *"This may turn out to be quite a nostalgic night for me."*

"Is there any place to get food close by?" Sean continued.

"Uh, well, I guess I could make a run to the 7-11 down the street. Do you— does Mark have any money on him?"

Sean shrugged. "Cash, no, but ..." He thought deeply for a moment. "I'm pretty sure his checkbook is in the inside flap of his sketchbook. I'll make sure, and then we can go with you."

Sean got past Alex and into the living room before he finally reacted. "Whoa! Whoa, hold it! I don't think that's a very good idea."

"I understand your concern, Alex," Alistaire told him, *"but you need not be alarmed. Sean and I are fully aware of the forms we occupy, and we have at least a working knowledge of our hosts' normal behavior. We will mind our manners."* He smiled. *"I admit to my own desire for a breath of night air. Whether I will be able to eat or not, I look forward to learning, and I, too, would not mind a short walk."*

Sean, who now had Mark's checkbook and I.D., spoke up. "If it makes you that nervous, lad, we'll stay. But we *would* like to go."

Alex swallowed hard, his eyes dancing from the floor, to Alistaire, to Sean, and back again. The thought of taking responsibility for the duo's actions out on the town rattled him no matter what reassurances they offered. I felt for him, but Alistaire *did* want to go for a walk outside, so Alex unfortunately received no help from me. The only place Sean had ever gone with Lora was to bed, so this would be a first for him as well.

Alex wrestled with himself a few seconds longer, his hyperactive temperament causing him to fidget at light speed, then sighed and said, "Look ... I'll do it, but you guys have *got* to swear to me that you'll act ... normal."

"No problem for me, lad," Sean told him with a clap on the shoulder. "The full moon is a week away."

Alex offered him a half smile, then looked to Alistaire, who in turn nodded his promise. "Okay then," he said, "I guess you can just follow me."

The night dazzled Alistaire's senses. The wind carried the barest hint of chill without being truly cold. Insects buzzed about under the parking lot light, June bugs clicking along the pavement, moths and other flyers bouncing against the casing. The air swam with the presence of people — normal, mortal humans pulsing with life. Alistaire smiled his pleasure at sensing no others of his kind in the immediate area. He glanced up at the partially lit moon and basked in its cool lunar glow.

"You seem to really be enjoying this," Alex observed.

"Yes," Alistaire admitted. *"As much as I miss a warm, spring day, I confess that my enhanced awareness makes the night quite pleasing."*

"Which way, Alex?" Sean asked, but before Alex could answer, the Irishman held up his hand. "Wait, don't tell me. Let me see if I can find it from Mark's memory."

Alex motioned him forward. Sean grinned and started walking.

"He's headed in the right direction," Alex whispered to Alistaire as they followed at a slower pace.

"I am not surprised," the German remarked. *"I find I can pull more from Neil with each visit."*

"Are the two of you coming closer together?"

"In a way."

"I've noticed your journey here has been getting easier to handle as well. The hypnosis takes about half the time that it did when we started all this."

Alistaire acknowledged with a grunt.

They continued on in silence for a few minutes before Alex suddenly asked, "What's it really like being a vampire?"

Alistaire regarded him sternly.

"I mean, I understand it can be unpleasant with the blood hunger and all—"

"There is more to it than just that," Alistaire said, almost snapping.

Alex paused a second, then said, "Please, talk to me

about it."

Alistaire slowed his pace as he chose his words and reprimanded himself for his sharp reaction to the boy's understandable curiosity. Alex's last words also suggested he thought it would "help" Alistaire to voice his feelings on the subject. The mortal could not truly comprehend how one grew accustomed even to unpleasant things after five-hundred years.

"The lust of the vampire does not thrive solely on blood," he explained. *"Blood is our sustenance, the fuel of our undead existence. Blood is the heart of our craving, but not the end of our hunger. There is more."* He gathered his thoughts further, then continued. *"Some vampires, usually the young fledglings still grappling with the shadows of their former humanity and the ghosts of their prey, try to justify their actions to their victims, their peers, and often themselves. They invoke the* great cats *hunting the elk, and ask if one should condemn the beast for doing that which only comes natural. All creatures strive for survival, they argue, and vampires are no different. But they are, we are, and none of their damned denials change the truth. Vampires are much more than mere blood thieves, much worse. Vampires ..."* His hands clenched and released before him, a physical manifestation of his reaching for the correct phrase. *"Vampires are ... addicts. Fear addicts."* He nodded to himself — the term was acceptable. *"Vampires are willful pleasure seekers, like mortals who use narcotics with no inclination or desire to break free of their habit. Vampires feed as much on their victims' fear as on their blood."*

"I think I read something like that. Don't vampires need adrenaline in the blood or they can't—"

"No, no, nothing like that. Adrenaline gives a certain preferred flavor to the blood, but it is by no means a

necessity. What I am talking about has nothing to do with nourishment, at least not in the physical sense. Almost without fail, when a vampire moves in for the kill, regardless of whether it was an open stalk or a subtle, masquerade approach, the creature will intentionally expose itself for what it truly is. The fear inspired by the revelation can be quite ... exquisite." Alex's eyes widened. Alistaire noticed the reaction and waved it away. *"Relax, my friend. I have not been holding out on you. I have never taken a victim. But, as I do feed on postmortem human blood instead of animal blood, which would only sustain me for a short time, I must likewise make some concessions with fear. G-God may have given me a strong will, but only He is omnipotent. I admit I find it extremely distasteful, but even I must indulge my drives from time to time and savor the fear of others. If a vampire is young enough, I can sometimes quench myself as I exterminate one of them. Unfortunately, the emotions of older vampires distort and change too greatly to prove useful. So, on occasions as rare as I can make them, I have frightened mortals to taste their fear. For what it is worth, I try to terrorize only those who have harmed others. I have visited prisoners jailed for heinous crimes, an easy feat for one who can change into mist and appear invisible to security cameras. I try to console myself by remembering that they will be less likely to sin again after their release."* He smiled, but it was a weak effort. *"To the best of my knowledge, the great cats have no need for such ... pettiness."* He finally looked at Alex and asked, *"So, do you now have a better idea of what it is 'really like' to be a vampire?"*

Alex replied, "Yes," and looked away.

They spoke no further as they followed Sean the remainder of the trip to the convenience store. Alistaire stepped through the door and surveyed the half-dozen customers and rows of merchandise, deeply appreciating the more relaxed atmosphere compared to such stores in Pittsburgh and New York City. The lack of other vampires would provide poor hunting, but if he were to retire sometime this century, he would seriously consider relocating to the Midwest.

Walking slowly up and down the aisles, he pondered what kinds of food to try. Would he really be able to eat, even if he was borrowing my body to do it? He deeply hoped so. Of course, the last time he had eaten there had not been such a thing as a "7-11," and he found himself a poor connoisseur of snack food. Perhaps he should select a drink first.

Moving over to the refrigerator, he found an equally challenging variety from which to choose. Sean had already raided the beer end, but Alistaire had not much cared for ale even when he was alive. Finally he sighed and reached for the soft drink he had heard of the most frequently, a Coca-Cola.

By this point Sean had made all of his selections, which consisted of ready-made sandwiches, a bag of corn chips and some dip, and a twelve-pack, and set his pile on the counter.

"Hey, Mark," greeted the clerk, a heavy-set black man with a warm demeanor.

Sean, knowing Mark frequented the store, stole a sly peek at the older man's name tag and replied, "Hey, Jack, how are you tonight?"

Although Alistaire thought nothing of it, I found the exchange quite amusing — it was a real kick to hear Mark doing Sean trying to do Mark.

Jack, in the meantime, stared down at Mark's checkbook as Sean opened it. "You plannin' on paying with that, are you?"

Sean blinked. "Well ... yes, actually. Is there a—?"

Jack released an exaggerated sigh and shook his head. "Look, kid, I don't have anything against you personally, but I tried to tell you about this the last time you were in here. Your last three checks bounced, and the boss is raising a real stink. I can't cut you anymore slack than I already have."

Sean obviously did not know what to do or how exactly to behave or react. Alistaire glanced over at Alex, who had also heard the exchange, and the two of them headed for the counter.

"Uh ... I'm afraid I don't know what to tell ye right now," Sean stammered, his confusion causing his accent to slip. "If ye'd like me to—"

"What I'd like you to do, Mark, is pay your damn bill," Jack snapped, his disposition not so warm now. "I wouldn't be so pissed if you hadn't had the gumption to try writing another check tonight. Now what do I have to do, huh?"

"Pardon me." Startled, Jack whipped his eyes over to Alistaire, seeing him for the first time. *"How much does Mr. Hudson owe this establishment?"*

Jack was clearly thrown off by Alistaire's intervention and manner of speech, but he answered, "Close to sixty bucks, I'd say. And that's *not* counting our returned-check fees."

Alistaire opened my wallet. *"I have forty-two dollars here."* He placed the Coke beside Mark's items, then scanned the merchandise up front and arbitrarily added a beef jerky — no time to be choosey now. *"Alex, do you want anything?"* Alex shook his head. Alistaire turned back to the clerk. *"By my estimation, we have no more than twenty dollars' worth of food and drink on this counter. I will give you forty-two dollars for it. Consider the surplus a down-payment toward Mr. Hudson's outstanding balance. In exchange, I ask for no further hassle this evening. Does this sound acceptable?"*

Jack mused over the offer, staring hard at Sean while doing it. He might have been waiting for the other shoe to drop over this deal, or he might have been considering that it *was* better to get part of the money now rather than refuse them service and risk never seeing any of it. "Yeah," he muttered finally, his fingers racing over the register keys. "It's 'acceptable.' You," he indicated Sean, "don't come back in here until you have the rest of it, okay?"

Sean nodded, gathered up their stuff, and headed for the door.

As Alistaire handed over my money, Jack leaned forward and said, "Look, you're obviously Mark's friend or you wouldn't be doing this, but if you *really* want to help him out, talk to him and slap him out of whatever funk he's been in lately. He's sinking fast, you know?"

Alistaire exchanged a quick glance with Alex, then said, *"Thank you for your cooperation."*

"Hey, no problem. I hope he works it all out."

Sean offered them a crooked grin as they joined him. "Sorry about that, friends. I had no idea. Mark doesn't keep track of his balance in his checkbook."

Alex snorted. "Sounds like he doesn't keep track of it anywhere."

Alistaire said nothing. He knew that anything they said in front of Sean would in turn be heard by the party in question. Better to wait and discuss it with Alex in private.

They returned to the apartment without further comment on the matter. Alex asked them occasional questions that amounted to nothing of real importance. Sean returned to his usual light-heartedness and helped himself to a beer. Alistaire, for the most part, remained silent and kept to himself.

Back inside, they settled down in the living room, Sean and Alex tearing into the chips, and Alistaire placing his own food and drink on the coffee table before him. He faced them with more tension than he felt before a battle. They were food for mortals, no longer suitable for creatures like him. Of course, those were arguments that would have stopped him *before* he saw my reflection in the mirror.

Gingerly, timidly, he reached out and took the beef jerky. A quick pull along the plastic strip and the meat was in his hand. He lifted it to his nose and inhaled deeply. The aroma, especially as heightened by his senses, awakened sensations and memories from deep within him. Was this really what it was like to feel a normal craving for a normal meal? He found he had almost forgotten. Now the only question was, how long would he sit and stare at the thing before he tried it? Holding his breath, he opened his mouth to take a bite, but at the last second he hesitated. Maybe he should try the Coke first?

In the meantime, Sean relaxed back on the couch and idly picked up Mark's sketchbook. He flipped through a few pages. "Not bad. Hey, Alistaire, you ought to see how he draws you when you're on the loose."

"I will look through it when you are finished," the German said offhandedly, his attention focused on the jerky.

"Are you scared to try it?" Alex asked, sitting next to him. "Don't you think it'll work?"

"On the contrary, I am more afraid that it will *work. I long ago grew accustomed to not eating as you do. It is a fact of my existence. I fear that if I eat normally now, I may find my normal in*ability *to do so that much more ... disconcerting."*

"Mmm. Maybe you could look at this as a bit of the past, like seeing your reflection — a *memory*, not an experience."

Alistaire smiled. *"I appreciate the suggestion, my young friend, but I think you will agree that such an approach would be easier said than—"*

"No."

Alistaire and Alex turned as one. Sean sat on the couch as before, but his attitude was now anything but relaxed. He glared down in open horror at the art book still gripped in his hands.

"Sean?" Alistaire asked, his concern soaring as he tasted the mixture of frightened and angry emotions radiating from his friend. Sean's hands were starting to tremble so badly that the pages of the book were making an odd fluttering noise that reminded Alistaire of all things like the winged flight of a bat. *"Sean, what is it?"*

"No," he repeated, this time through tightly clenched teeth. "No, this isn't right. This canna be right!" He shot an enraged look at Alex. "They don't know what the hell they're talkin' about! They're *wrong!*"

Alistaire was on his feet now. *"Sean, you're not making any sense. What have you found in that book?"*

"This!"

Viciously, he shoved the book into Alistaire's hands. The German held his gaze on Sean for a moment, then looked down at the open pages. The two-page spread was a conglomeration of a woman in various stages of her wolf form.

"They're *wrong*, I tell ye!" Sean growled. "They don't know anything about her!"

"Sean—"

"It's a *lie!*"

"Sean, it is just an illustration!"

Sean grabbed Alistaire forcefully by the shoulders. It was more a gesture of desperation than threat, but the mere idea that Sean would behave in such a way was enough to stun the vampire.

"My sister is *not a werewolf!*"

With one more snarl of anguish, Sean shoved himself away from the German, threw the front door open, and raced out of the apartment.

"Mark!"

"Sean!"

Alistaire made to pursue, but by the time he rounded the doorway, Sean was already halfway through the parking lot. What disturbed him most was that he could smell the *change* about the Irishman. Of course, that would be an impossible feat in his host body, but it did not speak highly of his mental state.

"You're not just going to let him leave, are you?!"

"It would appear that decision has been taken out of our hands."

"I don't get it. What happened?"

"Sean saw Mark's drawings of his sister. Sean holds certain ... denials about her. He has never taken well to having them challenged, although I have never seen him react quite this forcefully."

"Will he be all right?"

"Mark? Yes, I believe he will be fine. Sean? I do not know."

Alex wiped the sweat forming on his forehead. "Shit, man, this is gettin' too weird, gettin' out of control. Look, Alistaire, this ... I need to talk to Neil. Would you mind leaving ... please?"

Alistaire turned toward him slowly. He seemed on the verge of protesting, then said, *"Of course. Whatever you feel is best."*

"Thanks."

Alistaire nodded, then spotted the beef jerky and Coke still sitting on the table. *"I did not get the chance to try my food. Somehow I find I no longer want to."*

"Uh, yeah. Well, I guess you just ..."

His voice trailed away as Alistaire walked to the center of the room, lowered himself to the floor, and closed his eyes.

"Okay. I'm going to count from—"

"Don't bother, Alex," I said as I sat up and rubbed my tired eyes. "He's gone. Man, will you please remind him to blink occasionally?"

"Neil, this is gettin' way out of hand. Did you see the way Mark reacted—"

"The way *Sean* reacted," I corrected as I peered out the door in the direction he had run. "And yes, I saw it."

"*No*, goddamn it, I meant the way *Mark* reacted! That's exactly what I mean. You and Mark act like you're forgetting that Alistaire and Sean aren't real!"

"Don't worry about me. I know the difference. But I'm starting to think you might be right about Mark. Wait!" On the far side of the parking lot lay an open field. Although it was poorly lit, I thought I could see someone walking back our way. I found myself wishing for the extra heft that Alistaire lent my eyesight. Regardless, it became clear soon enough that it was indeed Mark. Whether or not Sean was still in control, I had no way of knowing. "He's coming back."

He looked terrible. His face was haggard, his skin ashen, his eyes sunken. The last few yards to the apartment seemed to take the last bit of his strength, and he leaned heavily on the door frame when he finally reached us.

"Mark?" I asked.

"Yeah," he replied. "It's me."

Alex and I each took an arm and helped him to the couch, where he collapsed with a deep-winded sigh.

"Are you okay?" Alex asked him.

"I think so. Just really tired."

My turn. "Can you tell us what happened out there?"

He nodded. "Sean changed."

"He what?"

"He changed. He was so upset by being confronted about his sister — which is something we *really* need to look into — that he just had to *run*, and two legs weren't fast enough."

"How exactly did it happen? How did you regain control? Or did you just force it?"

He winced in pain. "Man, head's killing me. No, I didn't force it. To be honest, I don't think I could have tonight." Alex shot me a look on that note, but I ignored it. "He let me go. We were running into the field, and he just took off and left me behind. I saw ..." He closed his eyes and cleared his throat. "I thought I saw him leave. In wolf form. Took off into the night." He tried to chuckle, but it came out as more of a croak. "Trick of the eye, right?"

"Yeah," I said. "What else could it have been?"

"Yeah. Look, Alex, I'm really shot. Would it be all right if I crashed here tonight?"

"Sure."

"Thanks. This spot looks good." He fell over where he was.

"One more thing, Mark," I said as he closed his eyes again. "What was that all about at the 7-11 with your checks?"

"Oh, yeah. Thanks for paying that. I mean, thank Alistaire for using your money, and all that ... whatever. Don't worry about it. Just a deposit mix-up with the bank. Takin' care of it this week ..."

"Mark," I said flatly, "a sixty-dollar/three-check balance error?"

Mark didn't respond. He was already asleep.

"Ready to call it a night?" Alex asked.

"I guess so. We're not getting anything else out of him

this evening."

"You can stay, too."

"No, thanks anyway. I'll head home."

I gathered my things together and Alex walked me out to my car. As I slid the key into the door, he said, "That guy at the store was right, you know. Mark is sinking, and it's clear that we had no idea how fast."

I breathed deep. "I know."

"We're playing games with Pandora's Box here, Neil. Maybe you guys should lay off the hypnosis before someone gets hurt."

"Yeah. I think maybe you're right." I slid behind the wheel.

"One more thing," Alex said before I closed the door. "Maybe I should read some more of your hypnosis book, in case things ever get weird and you're not around. Can I borrow it?"

I reached into my jacket pocket and handed it over.

"Thanks. Go home and get some sleep. You look like shit."

I nodded, closed the door, and drove off, leaving Alex with my book and me with my thoughts.

XIV

The ball sailed through the air like a rocket, spinning around its axis as it hurtled toward its target. Sean ran with all the speed he could muster, but it was going to be close. At the last possible instant, he leaped from the ground and the ball slammed firmly into the palms of his outstretched hands. Thomas collided with him a second later, but it was too late. Sean had cleared the two trees, and he had made the catch.

"And he's got it!" Eamon cried, his arms raised in a victorious V over his head. "Sean Mallory makes the catch and the crowd goes wild!"

The three friends laughed and collapsed to the ground in a tangle of arms and legs. Sean spun the ball mockingly in front of Thomas' face, who in turn kicked him in the shin. The three fell flat on their backs and continued to laugh.

Sean, Thomas Cassidy, and Eamon Rourke had invented the game the year they met, when Sean and his older sister had come to live with their foster parents. It was a mix-mash of baseball, American football, real football, and rugby. They had never really named it, simply referred to it as "playing ball," and it beat any of the games Sean had learned before moving further from Dublin.

The trio of teenagers eventually calmed down and lay

happily in the late-afternoon sunshine. It was a wonderful, warm day, the type of day that could make even headstrong lads truly appreciate being alive.

"I think I'm going to ask Maureen to marry me," Thomas said idly.

"Don't be daft," Eamon chided. *"Ye're too young."*

"And I suppose once I reach yer ripe ol' age I'll have yer blessin, eh?"

"Actually," Sean cut in, *"he's hopin' for a chance to break her in himself."*

"Traitor!" Thomas called as he kicked at Eamon.

"Actually," Eamon corrected, *"I'm hopin' t' break in Mallory's sister first."*

"Traitor!" Sean and Thomas called together as they both kicked at him.

They chuckled a bit longer, then Eamon's mood sobered. "What'd ye think of the proposition?"

Sean and Thomas frowned. Eamon didn't have to clarify — they knew exactly what he was referring to. The previous evening, the young men had been approached by a stranger to their little village. He spoke of recruiting young fellows like themselves to fight for Ireland's true independence. He never mentioned specifics or actually came out and offered them anything, but they knew they had just met a recruiter for the IRA, and he wanted them to join. If they decided they wanted "to discuss the issue further," they were to meet him at the end of the week.

"I'm not sure what to think of it," Thomas said. *"It could be the authorities tryin' to trick us, to see how we react."*

"I don't think so," Eamon returned. *"My gut tells me it's real."*

"I don't like it," Sean said.

"What don't ye like about it?"

"I'm not talkin' about his offer, Eamon. I mean I don't like the IRA."

Thomas and Eamon looked at him in surprise. Thomas spoke first. "Don't ye want Ireland's liberation?"

"Of course I do! I just don't agree with terrorism as a way to achieve freedom."

"What other choice do we have, Mallory?" Eamon demanded. "The Brits aren't backin' off on their own!"

Sean shook his head. "I just wish there was a different way. I admit I don't know what it might be, but that doesn't change my feelings."

"I suppose ye'd rather us go about protestin' and demonstratin' and holdin' rock'n'roll concerts like they been doin' in the States," Eamon chastened, his voice dripping with sarcasm. When Sean gave no response, he sighed. "I take it this means ye won't be talkin' to the man."

Sean shook his head.

"Thomas?"

"I'm not goin' unless Sean goes with us."

Eamon sighed again. "I guess that means none of us are goin'." He glanced at the sun that was now creeping closer to the horizon. "I'm headin' home. See ye lads tomorrow afternoon."

"Aye."

"See ye then."

Eamon climbed to his feet and headed off. Sean watched him go for several minutes before speaking. "Do ye think he's angry with me?"

"Even if he is, he won't be for long," Thomas reassured him. "Ye know Eamon. It's fiery chaps like him that give the Irish our reputation. He loves t' fight, and the idea of gettin' to do it for a real cause appeals to him. He'll forget it by mornin', and by tomorrow afternoon he'll

be angry bout somethin' else."

"Yer right, as usual," Sean chuckled. "I don't know what we'd do without ye, Thomas."

"Ye'd all whither and die, I'm sure." He winked, then stole his own glance at the sun. "We'd better be headin' home ourselves." He stood and offered a hand to Sean, who took it and joined him on his feet. "After you."

They walked in the opposite direction from Eamon. Sean and Thomas lived closer together than either of them to their friend, and they often found themselves out of his company after their days of fun. This evening they walked quietly, merely enjoying the fresh air and one another's presence. In many ways, Sean and Thomas had more in common. Both were less hot-headed, and hot-blooded, than their friend — more what the girls in school referred to as "nice," whereas Eamon was the lad about whom their mothers had warned. Eamon's remark about Sean's sister was only half in jest — good friend though he was, Sean always kept a watchful eye on him when Theresa was around. However, a few girls were beginning to notice Sean's rapidly developing rugged good looks, and Eamon insisted that Sean's day was just around the corner.

At last they reached the summit that marked the split of their journey home. Thomas turned right without pause and called, "See ye tomorrow!" over his shoulder.

"Thomas, wait a second!" Thomas stopped and looked back. "Ye never really told us whether or not you wanted to see the man."

Thomas shrugged. "I was curious what more he had to say, but it doesn't really matter."

"Thank ye, Tom. I won't forget this."

Thomas smiled. "I know." He waved and continued on his way.

Only a kilometer or so remained between himself and

home, so Sean moved at a casual pace. The sun finally dipped below the earth a few minutes later, and the stars twinkled into view. It was as clear an evening as it had been a day, and they were completely visible. The stars ...

... and the moon.

Sean looked up into the sky and breathed deep. Ahh. The reasons to take his time continued to add themselves to the list. His foster parents were abroad, and Theresa wouldn't scold so long as he made it home within the next hour or so. The night was turning out so gorgeous! The hills were well lit by the light of the full moo—

A sudden sharp pain shot through his head. He flinched and lifted his hand to massage his temple. Where had this headache come—

Another lightning flash brought him to an abrupt halt. He convulsed once, then twice as the searing needles shot through his neck, down his back, and finally out to his limbs. The pain was quickly joined by fear at the forefront of his thoughts. What was wrong? What was happening to him?!

The next spasm sent him to his knees, and he started to black out. He was aware of a ripping noise, and a deep, growl-like moan that reminded him vaguely of his own voice...

Then nothing but darkness.

*   *   *

Thomas whistled to himself as he climbed the hill that would bring his home into view. His mood was light despite thoughts of the evening's tension between Sean and Eamon. Then again, he was well used to it. It was a shame that the two butted heads so often. He knew they loved each other deeply, but their views and opinions about anything and everything could not have been more opposed. And more often than not, Thomas ended up playing referee.

Referee? Peacekeeper? He smiled to himself. Maybe he wasn't cut out for the IRA after all.

A small gust of wind met him as he topped the ridge. Unfortunately for Thomas Cassidy, the wind was not alone.

The thing struck him with such force that the actual impact blurred into non-existence for Thomas — one moment he stood looking toward his home, the next he lay flat on his back, the breath knocked thoroughly from his body. His vision darkened, and it had nothing at all to do with the time of day. He held his arms out in a dazed attempt to defend himself.

Thomas Cassidy never even saw the beast that killed him.

*   *   *

The first thing that came to his mind when he heard the moaning was: "That sounds like an awfully sick cow."

Not that he could remember ever hearing a sick cow, but somehow the association made sense. A lot more sense than the aggravating, chilly dampness that clung to one side of his body — he supposed he should open his eyes and try to figure that one out, too.

Sean raised his lids gently but had to shut them again when the bright light of dawn slammed into his sleep-sensitized pupils. His naked body shivered, causing gooseflesh to creep all over him. Better to simply curl up into a little ball of warmth, keep his eyes closed, and let the sick cow, the one that sounded enough like himself to be a reincarnated relative, moo away ...

All right. Let's sneak a quick look at that list.

There was no cow, of course. He was the one moaning. It was dawn, but the last thing he remembered clearly was walking home at sunset.

He was lying outside, on the grass.

And as near as he could tell, he was buck-naked.

All right, Mallory. Canna put this off any longer, lad. Time to open yer little eyes and figure out what the hell is going on.

Begrudgingly, Sean opened his eyes a second time. Sure enough, his blind man's assessment of his current situation was dead center. Well, almost dead center. He was naked, and lying on a grassy rise that his quickly roving eyes guessed to be reassuringly close to his home. The morning sun had yet to bid its farewell kiss to the fartherest reaches of the horizon. And a sharp catch of his breath confirmed that he was, indeed, the ill bovine.

The one little note that his sight-impaired imagination had missed was that he was covered in blood.

Releasing another moo, *this time one that spoke of a cow filled with fright rather than sickness, Sean tottered to his hands and knees. The sticky, crimson stuff covered a good deal of his upper body. On the side of his body that had faced upward as he lay, the blood had met with the dew and the result was a maroon shine that at once nauseated him. Had his hands not been equally coated, he would have covered his mouth firmly in his effort to avoid retching. As things were, he had to make do with a simple tightening of his lips ...*

... which led to his realization that his mouth was awash with blood as well.

The vomit came after all.

*   *   *

"Theresa!"

The panic-stricken plea brought the young woman to her feet in an instant. The cry was followed moments later by her younger brother crashing through the front door of their little home, his body devoid of clothing but covered in blood. Tears streamed down his face, and his limbs trembled in emotional anguish.

"Theresa, help me, please!" he wept. "I-I-I don't know what to-to—"

Heedless of the clammy mess coating his body, Theresa strode across the room and took him into her arms.

"Shh," she doted quietly. "Sean, I'm sorry. I thought I had more time. I waited too long." She gently led him toward the washroom. Thank God the foster parents were away! "We'll get you cleaned up, and I'll tell you everything."

Near collapse, Sean gave in gratefully to her maternal care while she cleaned him and told him about their father.

*   *   *

While Theresa strove to soothe Sean's state of mind, Eamon strode across the open lands toward Thomas' home. He had thought long and hard all night, and he'd be damned if he'd let an opportunity to aid their motherland slip away. If Sean was henpecked on the matter, then so be it, but Eamon had the distinct feeling that Thomas sidestepped the issue to run blocker for their timid friend. If he could speak candidly to Thomas for just a few ...

Eamon's thoughts fell into arrest, as did his breathing. He could only gape in horror at the sight before him.

A few yards ahead lay the remains of Thomas Cassidy. His guts — those that had not been grossly consumed — rested in strings across his lap and legs. His throat was an open cavity, bitten not across the windpipe, but lengthwise from chin to sternum, leaving a relatively shallow but long valley in his flesh. The tendons on his neck, now visible, were still taut from when he had probably tried to scream.

Eamon did not turn away, nor did he become ill. Instead, he merely stared at the bloody mess for several long minutes before breaking into a run for the Cassidy home.

*   *   *

"Just a little longer, Sean," Theresa whispered to him, tightening her grip on his arm. "Just hold on a little longer, then we'll be out of here, all right?"

Sean allowed himself something similar to a nod. Aside from that, he clung tightly to the numb mask that was the only real thing keeping him together as they lowered Thomas' body

*

painfully slow, the blood washed away

"why, Theresa"

"I canna say, Sean. it came through our father's side. sometimes it skips a generation. mother hoped it would pass over ye"

"no, no, I don't understand, how can this be"

"Sean, be still. breathe deep"

"I canna breathe deep. I smell it. don't you? the stink fills my nose and God help me I like it and"

"Sean, be still. ye must be clean in case someone comes"

painfully slow, the blood washed away

*

as they lowered Thomas' body into the ground. Theresa had convinced him that it would have been suspicious for them not to attend the funeral. After all, Sean and Thomas had been close friends for many years, and one never knew who might be "superstitious" enough to have their curiosity raised. The fact that it was the twentieth century, she told him in that knowing way, was not as much protection as they

*

wrapped the towel around him

he held his tongue a few seconds more, then he had to ask

"Theresa, do ye have it, too"

she just looked at him for a moment, then a loving smile warmed her face

"no, Sean.   for better or worse, for reasons I canna comprehend, it only passes on to the men"

despite his situation, he felt intense relief, but

*

not as much protection as they might like to think.

The crowd began to break up. With relief, Sean allowed himself to be led away from the scene. His comfort turned to panic when Theresa abruptly halted.

"What?" he whispered intensely, trying to keep the break out of his voice. "What is it?"

"We should probably say at least a word or two to his parents, just to be on the—"

"No." A sharp look from his sister told him to lower his voice. "No, Theresa, please, I can't."

"Sean, we—"

"I can't."

"All right, all right.   Listen, just stay right here for a moment. I'll speak to them and make yer excuses. Just stay right here and keep yer eyes lowered. Talk to no one, Sean. I'll be right back."

He shuddered as her warm hand left his arm, but he

preferred to hold his own amidst casual acquaintances than to have to face Thomas' parents

*

"Theresa, please don't say this"

"I have to, Sean. ye've got to accept what ye are if we are to make it, and that means accepting the whole reality of it. now, as I said, it's obvious ye hunted someone last night. I'm sure we'll learn who it was soon enough. we have"

*

to face Thomas' parents here and now. He couldn't do it, not if he wanted to ...

An icy hand fell over his heart and landed like a rock in the pit of his stomach. A few steps away, alone and heading straight for him, he spotted Maureen, the young girl Thomas had claimed he would marry.

God help me please I canna face her please ...

"Hello, Sean," she spoke when she stood before him. "I'm sorry, were ye prayin'?"

"Sort of. No matter."

"I wanted ... I'm glad to see ye, Sean," she said. Her voice was husky and her eyes puffy and red, but she held a tight rein on her emotions. "Thomas thought the world of Eamon, but it was you whom he really—"

Something inside him began to slip, and in spite of his greatest efforts, words began to flow from his lips.

"Maureen, I'm so sorry. Please forgive me."

"Forgive ye, Sean? Whatever for? Ye have nothing to apologize for. Ye were Thomas' best friend, Sean, and he knew it. Thomas loved ye more than

*

he looked up as she entered the room, the special room below the basement

"I still canna believe that this has been here all this time. do our foster parents know about this? they must"

his voice failed him as he noticed the look upon her face

"oh, no. ye found out who it was"

"yes, Sean"

"tell me, Theresa. I have to know"

"Sean, maybe ye should"

"tell me"

"all right. I'm sorry, Sean. a few hours ago they found

*

Thomas loved ye more than anything else in the world. Ye never brought him anything but—"

The tears flowed now. "Maureen, don't ye understand? It's my fault. I-I'm t-to blame. I—"

"I'm afraid Sean blames himself a little, Maureen," Theresa said as she spun her brother around and pressed his face against her to quiet him. "He was the last to see Thomas, and feels he should have been able to do something. I've told him it's silly, but I'm afraid he needs a little time."

Maureen drew a slow breath and touched Sean on the shoulder. Theresa bid farewell and condolences to her and hurried her brother away. Maureen watched them go, then went to find her parents.

A dozen paces away, Eamon thought about what he had heard. He thought about it hard, and the well of anger within him began to shift and find direction, and purpose.

*   *   *

The door to the lower level of the basement creaked a bit as he pushed it open. No matter. He would not have been stupid enough to inspect the house while Sean or Theresa were anywhere near it.

The room was dank, and dark. The light from the main basement bled through the opening, but he was still glad he had thought to bring an electric torch. He descended the wooden steps and played the light about the cellar. No windows could reach a room this far down, and there were no furnishings of any kind. The room smelled odd, as well. It reminded him of—

The light reflected off of something against the far wall, and he rushed forward to examine it. He found several chains in a pile on the floor. He pulled one free from the pile and followed its first end to a solid anchor at the base of the wall. These were thick chains, heavy chains. He traced it to the other end and found an equally imposing manacle. Running his fingers through it, he felt something more and held his findings up into the torchlight. He grunted. His months-long amateur surveillance had finally reached its apex.

Animal hair.

Eamon's eyes glistened with knowing and malice.

*   *   *

Sean ran for his life.

The crowd, not close behind but not nearly far enough away, pursued.

How did it come to this? *he thought.* Eamon ...

In dire need of rest, Sean dove over a small rise and buried himself in the high grass. The sun had dropped below the horizon a few minutes earlier, and he now saw the light of their torches shining all about, searching for his trail.

"Couple'a small details they forgot," he said bitterly to himself. "They should be carryin' flame torches and chantin', 'Kill the beast, kill the beast.' "

Lowering his head and breathing heavily, Sean desperately tried to find some new angle, some clue that might save his life. These were the facts as he figured them:

Somehow, over the last few months, his friend, Eamon, had discovered that he was a lycanthrope. Eamon then rounded up every superstitious simpleton across the countryside who had suffered property or live-stock damage to anything even remotely resembling the work of a wild animal (Sean was responsible for none of these actions, but try telling them that!). Those who believed Eamon — and, as Theresa had warned, they were a more numerous lot than he would have guessed — now followed him in search of their evil monster.

One item in his favor: The group that did agree to chase him down most likely didn't want the rest of the country to think they were mad, so at least Sean probably wouldn't have to worry about surprise reinforcements. The group of twenty or so slowly approaching him with their guns and blades, as nasty as that alone seemed, were the only threat loose on the moors tonight.

He could only guess why Eamon was doing this. Eamon found Thomas' body. Gossip of exactly how it was dismembered took no time in reaching Sean. If Sean had found a good friend's corpse in such a state, only to later learn that another, not-quite-so-close friend might be a budding werewolf ...

One question, and a vital one at that: As painful as he assumed it would be if they found him, were they really a mortal threat to him? After all, he was a werewolf. What were the odds on your average citizen possessing the proper arsenal to deal with such creatures? Maybe in their haste to hunt him down, they had forgotten ...

No. Eamon was many things, but he was not *stupid.*

Delude himself as he may try, Sean knew better than to underestimate his former friend. Even as he watched the mob, he caught the occasional shimmer of their blades, and some of those little sparkles seemed to pierce at his eyes, making it so he did not even want to look at them. How long had Eamon been planning this? How much time had he taken to prepare?

Like it or not, at least some of those gentlemen were almost certainly armed with silver.

Sean's heart skipped a beat. The mob, which had slowly begun to spread out, suddenly converged and marched straight toward him. They had spotted his trail again.

Sean groaned. He knew that if he started running again, he would tire before long, and then they would have him. If he headed for home, he would lead them straight to Theresa, an option Eamon had apparently failed thus far to consider. He could not do that to his sister.

If he wanted to live, there was but one course available to him.

"No."

Yes.

"No! Never again!"

Ye've been lucky so far, but just how long do ye think it'll be before takin' Theresa hostage crosses Eamon's mind? Ye've known him for years. Ye knew he could do it.

Ye have no choice.

Sean closed his eyes. Tears ran down his cheeks.

And he changed.

*   *   *

"Are ye sure about this, Eamon?" one of the men, Richard, asked.

Eamon turned, ready to crush the flicker of doubt before it could spread and circumvent everything he had fought for, but then realized that the man was referring to their latest trail, not their mission.

"Pretty sure," Eamon told him. "Not too many people come this way, but someone *went through here recently.* Very *recently. It has to be Mallory."*

"Why is it, boy," another man began, and this time Eamon could tell by the tone that the real *doubt was being voiced, "that he doesn't just change into the monster and outrun us, or attack?"*

"Look up, ye fool!" Eamon snapped. Several pairs of eyes drifted toward the heavens. "Don't see a full moon tonight, do ye?"

A few sighed in relief, while others covered their feelings by laughing at the man whom Eamon had cut short with ridicule. The moment had almost passed when they heard it.

The howl sliced through the night like they intended to slice their prey with their blades of silver. It was a deep, frightening sound that surrounded them, coming from all directions at once. The mob froze, sweat breaking out on more than one forehead despite the chilly air.

"Listen, boy," the ridiculed man said to Eamon, though without much satisfaction. "Don't know of any dogs *that bellow like that, do ye?"*

Eamon shot him a harsh glance, but his attention was on the land around them. Those with torches waved them back and forth, their light beams searching in vain. Eamon did not like this at all. How could Mallory transform without a full moon? While he had formed his little army, he had chuckled to himself more than once at the imbeciles who actually harbored secret beliefs in the legends — at least Eamon had researched his notion before allowing himself to accept it. Now he wondered whether he was as foolish as those around him. Just because the heart of the myth had turned out to be true, why did he assume that every aspect of it could be trusted?

"Damn," he cursed, and gripped his blade tightly as a second roar filled the night. Wherever Sean was, he was drawing closer. "All right," he said. Young though he was, they had accepted him as leader thus far. "Let's, uh ... let's back into a tight circle. Those with the silver blades try to spread yourselves out—"

A rifle fired. A scream. A large, dark form barreled through them, knocking many to the ground, and almost all off-balance. Eamon slashed at the shape as it passed by him, but the effort was a futile expression of rage, as he missed by no less than ten feet.

"Oh, God, Ian!" someone screamed. The man stood, blood dripping from his face, the spray from his friend's chest wounds continuing to dampen his trousers. The man screamed again, dropped his rifle, and fled into the night.

"Ye idiots!" Eamon yelled.

No one was listening.

The rifles began firing again. In the panic, one man shot another in the shoulder. With the exception of Eamon, although even he was starting to feel like he was lost in a dream, hysteria swept the whole lot into its frenzied embrace. All hell was breaking loose.

Just like Sean had hoped.

With the man who had fled lying dead on the ground before him, Sean lingered now in the darkness, watching for another opportunity to dive through their midst. He tried to ignore the elation, the swell of energy, the sheer exhilaration of using his power, his gift, his curse. While it had been a tremendously large but otherwise normal-looking wolf that had attacked the circle of men moments earlier, the form he now held crossed characteristics of both man and animal. Rather than standing on all fours, his hind legs and back had straightened enough to allow him to rise to a low crouch, with a pair of clawed hands rather than paws resting on his knees.

His senses were only marginally less sharp in his new form. He could see the men, stumbling about and firing at random into the shadows. He could hear their quickened breath, and he could almost swear he heard a racing heartbeat or two. Most of all, he could smell them, their sweat, their blood, their fear. All except for Eamon. Eamon, his friend for years, stood amongst them, the only one studying the surrounding gloom with careful scrutiny, and he reeked not of fear but of hate.

Sean sadly shook his enlarged, snouted head.

Eamon wanted to throttle the lummoxes around him as they shot at the slightest gust of wind, but he bit his tongue. Who knew? If Sean could transform outside of the full moon's cycle, if he could actually control the beast — a possibility that now seemed very likely, considering the wolf's latest actions, and that served to build on Eamon's hatred even more — who was to say he couldn't be taken down by a bullet of lead as well as silver?

A glimpse of movement from the corner of his eye — he spun, lifting his blade.

Sean raked his claws across Eamon's shoulder. The young man cried out and attempted to counter the assault, but Sean vaulted out of his range. Baring his teeth, Sean tore into the men who proposed to take his life.

The first wound he suffered from a normal, steel knife. Feeling it slash into his side was an odd sensation. Not at all pleasant, but not the whetted pain that it should have *been. He felt the blade break the skin, enter his body. It reminded him of when his dentist had pulled two of his bottom teeth — his mouth had been numbed, of course, but he could still feel the doctor's movements, the tug and pull at his gums. Not something one cared to experience every day. As he moved forward and the knife withdrew, he felt the muscle and tissue instantly begin to heal. Perhaps there were some benefits to being a werewolf after all.*

The second injury was from a blade of silver. While the first caused Sean to realize just how much his sensitivity to normal harm had diminished, this new strike was unlike anything he had ever felt, or imaged he could feel, in his life. The cut, two inches long but barely deep enough to break the surface, fell across his wrist, but the searing needles of anguish lanced through his arm past the elbow and almost to the shoulder. While the first cut had compared to having teeth pulled under novocaine, this was like biting tin between two fillings, an almost "sweet" pain that ached into the very bone. He screamed-roared, and took guiltless pleasure in disemboweling the man who had wounded him.

The last successful strike came near the end of the confrontation. Almost all of the men were dead now. Sean had made sure to kill every one of them for two reasons: To hopefully protect himself and his sister from a second such mob, at least in the near future, and as a caution against spreading his lycanthropy — he might have inherited it, but even Theresa admitted she didn't know whether or not it could be spread to another by his bite. Ironically, at least three of his enemies had fallen under the bullet of one of their own comrades.

Sean pinned one of his last opponents to the ground, biting into his neck to end his life and his screams, when his nostrils suddenly burned with a new odor, one he identified almost immediately as kerosine. An instant before he could turn, he felt heat and then the scorching lick of flames across his lower back. He reeled away from the source.

Standing on all fours, the canine equivalent of a grimace on his face and smoke rising from the fur on his hind quarters, he faced his final adversary.

Damn, Eamon. He did *bring a flame torch!*

"Come on, ye bastard," Eamon spat, the torch held high in one hand, his silver dirk in the other.

Keeping his guard up, Sean reverted into a more human form. Eamon's eyes widened. In a matter of seconds, Sean Mallory stood before him — his body a little hairy, his teeth a little long, his fingernails a little sharp, but Sean nevertheless.

"So I was right," Eamon smirked. "Ye can *control yerself. That just makes ye all the more the devil! What happened, Sean? Did Thomas annoy ye with an odd word, or did he make one joke too many about yer sister? That never brought ye tearin' down on* my *throat!" He jabbed the knife forward for emphasis.*

Unimpressed, Sean returned, "To hell with ye, Eamon! I didn't know what I was doin', but I make no excuses! And I bear my grief for it!" Eamon snorted hatefully at that, but Sean ignored him and continued. "Have I done anything like it since? If not for you *and yer actions tonight, I might never have taken a human life ever again!"*

"But ye have, haven't ye, devil!"

"I warn ye, Eamon," Sean said slowly, his voice deepening again, his chest thickening and his back hunching. "I may feel guilt, will probably feel it for the rest o' my life, but make no mistake! I am not a paralyzed invalid jumping at every quake in the air about me, as I'm sure ye've seen tonight. If I could make it through Thomas' funeral, I can face anything. Somehow, someway, I'll try to

make amends of all this, then I'll face God when the time comes and He'll judge me as He sees fit. But I will not be judged by the likes of you!"

"Then face me, hell spawn!" Eamon laughed. "I'll send ye before His judgement right now!"

Allowing Eamon to goad him, Sean leaped upon him in his current barely-wolfman form ... and he paid for his mistake. The flames scorched the side of his head while the silver blade punctured his chest, glancing off a rib directly over his heart. Then Eamon laughed, and his arrogance tilted the balance again. Despite the pain, Sean shifted back into his full wolf form and raked his hind legs down Eamon's front.

The former friends fell away from one another. Sean cradled himself as best he could in wolf form. The burns ached terribly, but they were nothing compared to the silver wound in his chest. Actual damage notwithstanding, he honestly did not know if he could survive this horrible agony!

Eamon staggered about, blood quickly soaking through the tattered remains of his clothing. He looked down at the long slashes running from his chest to his knees, then lifted his gaze to Sean. He seemed about to say something, but then his eyes rolled back in his head. He dropped the torch, which fell into a pool of blood on the ground and started the coughing and flickering that would eventually lead to its burning out. The silver blade dangled from a leather strap which Sean had not noticed before — a strap tied around Eamon's wrist, no doubt, to prevent his disarmament. Finally, Eamon collapsed, drew two choking gasps of air, then stopped breathing altogether.

Sean looked about himself, unable to believe it was really over. How long had it actually taken? he wondered. Probably a few minutes, but it felt much longer to his stinging, throbbing body.

What should he do now? It wasn't as if he could hide this carnage, but should he just leave them as they were? What would the rest of the country think? Would those who first laughed at Eamon now lift a call of alarm? How much protection could a mythical creature hope for from the age of science and logic?

Sean finally decided that, regardless, he was incapable of doing much in his current state. For better or worse, he had better reach his home while he still could, and deal with the repercussions later.

He limped to the remains of his own clothing a few dozen yards away, gathered them up in his maw, and moved as quickly as his four tired legs could carry him toward home.

When he finally disappeared, Eamon released the breath he had been holding. The long scratches down his body smarted terribly, but that was all they really were: Deep scratches. Sean, in his pain, had missed his mark, but that still did not make it wise to go toe-to-toe with a werewolf. Eamon was not stupid.

Moving as quietly as he could, hoping the pain dulled Sean's senses as it had his aim, Eamon followed him.

*   *   *

Sean stumbled through the door of his home. All was quiet and dark.

"I'll be damned," he muttered with a humorless smile. "She wasn't home to begin with."

Dropping his clothes into a pile on the floor, he limped on now human feet into the lavatory. The burns across his back and face were already starting to heal, if a bit slower than his steel knife wound, but the silver gashes hurt more *than ever. He bathed them with water — he knew he should probably try alcohol, but one thought of that additional sting turned his stomach. Good for him or not, he wasn't masochistic enough to do that to himself just yet.*

Foregoing the modesty of even a towel about the waist, he moved to his bedroom and fell upon the comforting mattress. Sleep reached up for him.

A moment before he drifted away, a sound from outside drifted to his ears. He lifted his head and breathed deep through his nose.

Eamon! *Somehow, the bastard had survived and followed him home!*

Sean strained to rise from the bed, to face his foe once more and end it one way or another, but his body betrayed him. His fatigue was so great he could neither stand nor sprout a single wolf hair.

I suppose this is it, then, *he thought, then surrendered to the darkness.*

* * *

Eamon waited a few minutes after Sean entered his home. If he gave the devil time enough to fall asleep, that would give him the advantage he needed. He counted the time as patiently as he could, then gripped his silver knife and advanced.

He stopped a few feet from the front door. He half-expected a moment of reflection, of old feelings for Sean to flash through his mind. Nothing happened. The image of Thomas' body burned too brightly in his memory.

"To hell with ye, Mallory."

He stepped forward ...

* * *

Sean bolted awake when Theresa laid the wet cloth across his forehead. A gentle hand on his shoulder prevented him from rising. Vertiginous with fever, he closed his eyes.

"Lie still, Sean," she whispered to him. "Ye were wounded by silver, weren't ye?"

He managed a nod.

"It'll take time for ye to heal from this," she told him. "Ye must rest for a few days."

"Theresa," he began, but her name came out as a dry croak. He cleared his throat and repeated himself. "Eamon followed me here. Where—"

"Shh." She rested her fingers over his lips. "I've taken care of everything, Sean." He looked at her, his eyes wide. She nodded.

Sean's gaze drifted past her, through the open door into the living room, to the rifle hanging over the hearth. He then closed his eyes. At least it was over.

A knock sounded at the door. Theresa covered him with a sheet and left the room, pulling the door to but not closing it. A few seconds later, Sean heard her speaking to Samuel, one of their closer neighbors. They exchanged words casually, and Sean soon found himself drifting away again.

He was brought back from his stupor when Samuel poked his head into the room.

" 'lo, lad," the middle-aged man said with a smile. "How ye feelin'? Yer sister tells me ye're ailin'."

Sean nodded.

"Listen, I know this probably isn't the time, but I feel ye have a right to know." Samuel stepped into the room hesitantly. "Theresa's outside with the wife. I don't know if she'd tell ye herself just now, but like I said ..." He swallowed. Sean listened. "Sean, I'm afraid that Eamon

boy ye stick with was killed last night."

Sean was grateful for his obvious illness. It saved him from having to act the part of shock or grief with any vigor.

"I know ye lost yer other friend not long ago," Samuel continued. "When ye're well, ye come talk to me. A bunch of us're talkin' of forming a huntin' group to track this thing. Seems a bunch of men from around here decided to have a little party last night. Eamon was with them. They were out in the middle of nowhere drinkin' away when this thing must've hit them ..."

Samuel continued talking, seemingly to himself now, but Sean's thoughts raced to the point where he heard very little. Out drinking? What the hell was Samuel talking about? Those men had no liquor with them. And where was the talk of rifles and knives? Surely that would be the most prominent of gossip at a time like this! What had Theresa said? That she had taken care of everything? What the hell did she do, go out there and take all their weapons while planting alcohol on them?! For God's sake...

Then Samuel's next words penetrated his haze, and his heart stopped. "Of all the lot, Eamon had it the worst! That creature must have had a taste for young men, I'll say! The beast tore that boy limb from limb with such fervor they had trouble identifyin' him! I know when ye're well ye'll want to join us when we ..."

Sean stared wide-eyed at the babbling man, then looked to his sister, who now stood in the doorway. She returned his gaze without wavering, her face unreadable. She then stepped out of sight.

No. No, no, no, no, no ...

FIFTEEN

"... so you're saying that a stake through the heart would *not* hurt you?"

"Not exactly. What I am saying is that the myth of the wooden stake became a double-edged sword well before my time. There are many legends that vampires have encouraged, such as the ridiculous notions of our abhorrence to garlic and running water, to the end of misleading mortals into a false sense of security, to defending themselves with worthless trinkets. However, some of the legends have grown over such a long period of time that even the vampires *cannot recall if they are based in fact or fiction. For instance, Mikhail, the very vampire who cursed me, went to great lengths to coerce a* formal *invitation into my home, while I myself have never found the need for such ceremonious consent. The penetration of a stake through the heart is another dilemma. I feel it is reasonably safe to assume that not just* any *wood could do the job, but what about oak specifically? Or ash? In this case, the myth has become its own animal. I personally have never heard of any vampire successfully destroyed in this manner, but the enigma still remains. Is* it truly a *threat? The only way to answer that question would be to put the legend to the test, and as you may imagine, there are precious few vampires willing to volunteer. So the myth*

*stands. Whether or not the danger genuinely exists, my kind
of undead have no choice but to treat the stake as the threat
it may be and act and defend ourselves accordingly."*

Jimmy nodded. So did Kathy, Mike, and Chris.

Deathtrap had closed, the next big party had arrived,
and — despite some misgivings from me over the recent
developments with Mark — Alistaire had kept his word.
This time Chris offered to play host, since his parents were
away in Europe, and cast and crew members and their
assorted friends moved through the house laughing and
chatting and drinking. Unlike last time, the party as a whole
had not been interested in the exhibition, but Kathy had
insisted, so down I went and up rose Mr. Bachman.

In some ways it was a little annoying. After all, I was
looking forward to spending time with Kathy away from the
theatre, and perhaps getting a little closer to her — I couldn't
exactly do that while playing the stoic German vampire.

As time had passed, I'd grown increasingly attracted to
Kathy. I enjoyed chatting with her about anything and
everything, and it didn't take long to discover that we shared
the same viewpoints on many different subjects. On top of
all that, she was *very* sexy, with an athletic tone to her body
that clothing could not hide. Her dark hair and features,
emphasized by diamond blue eyes, fueled more than one of
my dreams. The fact that she was three years younger than
me mattered little, at least as far as *I* was concerned. Age,
however, was not my main deterrent.

Her brother Peter proved to be more and more of a
hindrance as I tried to get closer to her. Personally, I had no
problem with him — he was a little quiet, but it only
reminded me of how *I* had been before catching the acting
bug, and he'd been a great help during the run of the show.
Still, his constant presence whenever I saw her was getting
annoying. He shadowed her like they were joined at the hip,

and even the slightest innuendo from either of us ruffled his feathers. I could only guess how he would react if I actually made a move on her.

Another potential problem was her father. It had become clear as rehearsals for *Deathtrap* began to run late that Kathy and Peter's dad wasn't the most easy-going guy in the world. *He* was another reason why Peter always tended to be with her, especially whenever some of us went out. It didn't help my confidence that the community theatre people referred to him as "the Nazi."

Anyway, Alistaire had been chatting with Kathy and the others for almost an hour, and was genuinely enjoying himself. Unfortunately, at around eleven o'clock or so, things got a little off the beaten track.

Susan Tate and Dean Leitner arrived and entered the party with their usual, obnoxious fanfare. Susan and Dean had been the bad seeds of this year's Acting One classes, taking Theatre because it was supposed to be an easy "A." When the facts had been revealed otherwise, they'd shown their displeasure by disrupting class whenever possible — a typical high school reaction, but a little more offensive on the collegiate level. Still, they did know everyone, and partied often with more than one of my crew members. They'd never interrupted my rehearsals, and had shown up to one performance each, so I tolerated them. In my opinion, they'd never grown past the stage of thinking that *sarcasm* was the highest level of humor, but that was just *my* opinion, so I kept it to myself.

So, into the Barnes house they came, spouting their irritating witticisms left and right. Alistaire had only the vaguest notion of who they were and gave them little thought. Fifteen minutes later, as Alistaire was covering for Jimmy what was old ground for me, Dean found his way over to our little group.

"Hey, Barnes," he said too loudly, "what's up?"

"Nothin'," Chris said blandly, hoping he'd lose interest and wander away.

Dean did *not* wander away, but turned to look at Alistaire. "John said some shit about Carpenter here playing like a vampire, or some shit like that."

"Uh, not quite," Chris replied, and said nothing more.

Dean didn't take the hint. He stared at Alistaire with his usual insufferable grin, and the German quickly found that *he* did not care for Dean any more than *I* did.

"May I help you with something?"

Dean laughed a high-pitched shrill. "Nice voice. You get that stare from Hannibal Lector?"

Alistaire did not respond. He simply stared a hole through Dean. After a few seconds, the punk's cool facade began to slip. Then Mike asked, "Don't you have somewhere else to be?"

Dean muttered, "Assholes," and strutted away.

"Sorry about that," Kathy said.

"There's no reason for you *to be sorry, Ms. Schaumbur*g," Alistaire told her. *"I believe that* Trey *would score higher on an I.Q. test than* that *individual."*

The others got a kick out of that. They didn't realize that Alistaire was serious.

The respite lasted about five minutes before Susan Tate walked up behind Alistaire and pinched him on the butt. The German stiffened at the affront and turned to face her.

"Hey, Neil," she said, trying to look sexy through her thick mask of make-up. "Dean says you're being a real stuck-up prick tonight."

Mike, who liked her and Dean even less than I did, groaned, "Susan, why don't you just—"

"I wasn't talking to you, shithead," she bit. She smiled at Alistaire again and asked, "So, is Dean right? Are you gonna snob me tonight, Neil?"

Icily, even by his standards, Alistaire stated, *"I am particular about whom I choose as company."*

Susan simply cooed as if he had flirted with her. "Dean also said some bullshit about you pretending to be a *vampire* or whatever. What's that all about?"

"Susan," Chris spat, "get lost."

Susan laughed, rolled her shoulders, and tried to grab Alistaire's crotch.

That was the straw that broke the vampire's back. Alistaire's hand snaked out and locked onto her wrist. She yelped in surprise. *"If you would like to know what this is all about, I would be happy to* show *you."*

Susan looked into Alistaire's eyes and cringed in fear. She turned and cowered, hiding her face with her free hand.

Jimmy stuttered, "Neil, what the hell are you doing?"

"Alistaire, please," Kathy said, touching his arm, "just let her go."

Alistaire looked down at her, as she slumped onto her knees. What had he done? Over five centuries to build up an ocean of patience, and this girl had upset him with a mere touch? Had he become that sensitive to human contact? He quickly released her.

Susan pulled away and sat on the couch, crying. Those around the room who had no real idea of what had transpired stared daggers at Alistaire. Mike, Jimmy, and Chris had little sympathy, but Kathy at least offered to console her, trying to explain what it was I was doing, who Alistaire was and that she didn't really need to be afraid of him. Dean appeared and sat next to Susan, who still hid her face in her hands, her shoulders trembling. Kathy looked up at Alistaire apologetically.

Guilt bucking within him, Alistaire knelt before Susan. He reached out and took her hand.

"I am sorry," Alistaire told her sincerely. *"I lost my temper. I did not mean to frighten you."*

A brief instant before anyone could say or do anything more, Alistaire realized something. In his concern for having injured an innocent person, he had ignored what his senses told him. Susan groveled in fear, yet he smelled no perspiration on her, no scent of adrenaline leaking from her pores. Her heart beat at an even, barely elevated pace.

Susan's hand closed around his. She threw her head back ...

... and laughed.

"Goddamn, Neil," Susan howled, "you ain't *that* fuckin' good of an actor!"

Dean joined in with her, and they laughed at the German vampire whom they thought was me.

A dozen emotions coursed through Alistaire. He felt confused, annoyed, betrayed, embarrassed, apathetic, angry ... all at the same time. With a great deal of dignity, he rose to his feet and stepped through the front door, leaving Mike Dalton to tell Susan and Dean in no uncertain terms what pathetic human beings they both were.

Alistaire stepped out onto the front porch, his breath coming in long, controlled swells as he sat on the Barnes' porch swing. The night was pleasant, if a bit windy, and he stared out into the darkness.

A minute later, Kathy emerged from the house and sat down beside him. Alistaire also noticed Peter near the doorway, but her brother's constant watch didn't irk him as it did me. He simply ignored the boy.

"Are you okay?" she asked, smiling with her usual warmth.

Alistaire returned her affectionate gaze. *"I am fine. Perhaps a bit humbled. To coin a phrase, I allowed her to 'get my goat.' She should be commended, actually."*

Kathy raised an eyebrow. "Somehow, Mr. Bachman, I get the feeling that your thoughts toward Susan aren't really as gracious as you're pretending."

Alistaire smiled. *"Somehow, Ms. Schaumburg, I get the feeling that you are correct."*

They laughed together.

"Alistaire, may I ask you a question?"

"Certainly."

"I was wondering ..." She paused, then blushed. She faced outward so that he could only see her profile. "I hope this isn't cheating, asking *you* instead of ... well, I was wondering how Neil feels about me."

Alistaire regarded her. *"Why* don't *you ask Neil? Why ask* me?"

"I don't know. I'm not usually the shy type, but to be honest, I just feel more comfortable asking you about it. Oh, I understand the hypnosis and all that stuff, so I know it sounds silly ..."

"Katherine, you may be many things, but one thing that I am certain you are not *is 'silly'."*

"Really?" Kathy shifted again so that she faced him directly.

"Yes. Neil finds you quite beautiful, enchanting, delightful, engaging, alluring, attractive, and mature beyond your years. You are perfectly pleasant company, and, as Neil has foolishly procrastinated on telling you, allow me *to assure you that he would feel honored if he were allowed to court you sometime in the near future."*

Kathy appeared stunned. She found her breath and whispered, "Is this Neil's way of asking me out?"

"I am 'asking you out' for him."

She beamed at him and answered, "I would *love* to go out with Neil."

Alistaire nodded warmly.

Kathy breathed in, held it for a moment, then relaxed. "Well then, I'll see if I can get a night out without my brother as chaperon!" Grinning ear-to-ear, she squeezed his hand, then excused herself as she stepped back into the house.

Amazing, I thought. *Truly amazing.* Alistaire had found the courage to do in a few minutes what I had been hoping to do for *weeks*.

The front door opened again, and Susan and Dean emerged, yelling over their shoulders that they would be back with some beer. They were down the steps before Susan noticed Alistaire watching them from the swing.

"Hey, Neil," she cooed, "still sulking that I got you good?"

Dean cackled.

Alistaire curled the edges of his lips in a pale affectation of a grin, rose to his feet, and almost floated down the steps toward them.

"Yes," he said, and if his tone was cool normally and icy earlier, it was positively *sub-zero* now. *"You did 'get me,' didn't you?"*

He had their attention now, and this time neither of them was pretending.

"Hey, cool it, Neil, it was only a joke, okay?" Susan said, veiling her uncertainty with smugness.

"Yeah," Dean piped in, "don't be such an asshole."

"Oh, I don't mean to be an 'asshole,' my friend," he replied, his smooth footsteps carrying him closer to them even as they unconsciously backed away. *"As I indicated, you fooled me quite well. I allowed a silly thing such as legitimate concern for your well-being to cloud my judgement. But* please, *allow me to indulge in a little more of that same concern, and offer you both a little piece of advice."*

Susan emitted a tinny, involuntary squeak when her

behind hit the car Alistaire had backed them up against. Dean's eyes darted back and forth, as if looking for some means of escape from this snobby college Junior who had suddenly become completely demented before his very eyes.

"Y-yeah?" Susan spat, her final attempt at using sarcasm as a defense. "And what exactly is that?"

"I am a special case, as I heard Katherine explaining to you. But do yourselves a favor. If, in your short little journey through your short little lives, you ever happen to encounter another vampire along the way, don't ever, ever..." He leaned closer and lowered his voice for emphasis, *"... allow them to get this close to you."* He widened his eyes just a little, and drew back his lips, baring his teeth at them in dark pretense of a smile.

With speed and agility that defied their poor physiques, Dean and Susan leaped into their car and left long, black tread marks on the road in their urgency to get as far away from Alistaire as they possibly could.

Alistaire stared after them until they rounded the corner at the end of the street, then turned and headed for the house, his stride easier and lighter than before. After all, as he had recently confessed to Alex Monroe, if he were to successfully maintain his station in this unlife, he had to indulge himself, just a *little*, from time to time.

*   *   *

When the next Producing student moved into the Old Science Hall theatre, Mark agreed to help me strike the remains of my *Deathtrap* set. I was thankful for the much-needed assistance, but unfortunately, his offer turned out to be a preamble to his dropping a bit of a bomb in my lap.

I was taking a breather, sitting on the apron of the stage opposite Mark, who faced me from the house, when he suddenly spoke.

"Neil," he said heavily, "I, uh ... I'm in a little trouble." Now that he had my attention, he stared blankly at his hands for a moment before continuing. "I ... I guess I've sort of let things get away from me, somehow. I haven't been to any of my classes in a while, I haven't even finished drawing the last two pages of *The Triumvirate* yet." He chuckled then, at what exactly I wasn't sure. "It really has to do with money."

The incident in the 7-11 immediately flashed through my mind, but I said nothing.

"I've done a pretty shitty job managing my funds lately. Scholarships spent, loans overdue ... my mom isn't well off, can only help so much. Kept meaning to get a part-time job, but ..." He fell into silence, this time focusing his attention on the stage lights.

"How bad off *are* you, Mark?" I asked, not really sure I wanted to hear his answer.

"Pretty bad," he confessed. "Pretty bad off all around. Did you know Lora and ... and I broke up?"

I blinked and shook my head. I hadn't.

"Sorry, didn't mean to change the subject. Guess I'm so broke I can't even afford to pay attention." He tried to smile at his own joke, but the mood killed what small amusement the little pun might have given. "The Bursar's Office evicted me from my apartment, and they're holdin' all my belongings hostage until I pay the university the money I owe it. I've got hot checks in every fuckin' store across town. I'm hoppin' from convenience store to convenience store one check at a time, knowing I can't go back once they try to cash the damn things." He cleared his throat, then stood and moved from his front row seat to sit beside me on the stage. "I don't want all this to fuck you up, Neil. It looks like I'll probably be dropping out of school and moving in with my mom up in Tulsa. I was wondering, though, if maybe I could stay at your apartment for a couple of days."

I gripped his shoulder. "Of course, Mark. No problem."

At least he'd made no mention of Sean Mallory. That was something.

*   *   *

Two days later, I sat in the Green Room between classes, going over some notes for an upcoming final. It was one of those "off-times," when most people were still *in* class, so I shared the room with only two other people, and believe me, when the Green Room is actually that quiet, you take advantage of it.

I might have stayed enveloped in my notes for the next half-hour had I not glanced up long enough to see Lora walk past one of the doorways. I sat still at first, questioning whether I was over-stepping my bounds, then decided to hell with etiquette and bounded after her.

"Lora!" I called as I stepped into the hall. My voice brought her to a halt just before she rounded the corner. As I hurried to catch up with her, I asked, "You got a minute?"

She looked at me warily, then glanced at her watch. "I guess."

"Thanks." I fell silent as I fumbled for the right words, unsure of how to breach the subject. "I, uh, heard, that you and Mark broke up."

She stiffened. "Yeah," she told me, not bothering to hide the apprehension in her voice.

"Hey, Lora, relax," I said with what I hoped to be a charming grin. "I'm not here to come down on you or anything. I just, uh ... well, I don't mean to be nosy, but Mark was pretty vague about it, so I was wondering if maybe you could shed some light on it for me. Please."

She fidgeted around, her eyes looking everywhere

except at me. "What exactly do you want to know?"

"Well, uh ... I'm not sure, really. Just the broad strokes on *why* you broke up, I guess."

" 'The broad strokes,' " she repeated. Somehow the phrase sounded bogus and distasteful when she said it. Whatever my intentions, *she* clearly felt I was prying.

"Lora, I'm just worried about Mark. He's been acting—"

"Weird, yeah, I know." She finally looked straight at me. Tears peaked over the rims of her eyelids. "*That's* why we broke up, okay? He was getting just too fuckin' weird on me."

I sort of nodded. "I see. Did he start falling into Sean at odd times, or—"

"No, no, no," she snapped, waving away the notion with a sharp gesture. "That's not what I mean. Sean's never bothered me. Sean's sweet and kind and fun. He'd never do anything to hurt me."

"Uh, Lora, look, Sean isn't real, he's—"

"I *know* that!" she shouted, and for a second I thought she was going to shove me away from her. "I *know* he's not real! I'm not as *stupid* as everyone thinks I am!"

I started to respond, to deny any such opinion, but instead I bit my tongue and listened to what she was saying.

"I know Sean's just another side of Mark and his creativity and all that crap, all right? I *know* that! I also know that Sean's supposed to be a stupid werewolf and all *that*, okay? But Mark wasn't *doing* Sean that night!"

"What night?"

She got control of herself, probably because we were starting to draw some serious attention from the few people passing by. She wiped her eyes with the back of her hand and told me, "Last week, okay? Thursday, I think. We were together, me and *Mark*, not Sean. He freaked out on me."

"What'd he do?"

She shrugged and sighed. "He ... he didn't really *do* anything, he just ... freaked out, acted funny. Locked himself in the bathroom and told me to leave, not to come back. The next day he pretended not to remember much about it. 'All a little blurry,' he says. Bullshit. I'm tired of his moods. I told him to stay away from me. That's it, okay? Can I go to class now?"

"Yeah," I told her. "Thanks for telling me about it. I'm sorry ... you know."

I gave her a little hug, which she accepted rigidly, then let go of her so she could hurry upstairs to her dance room.

As she walked away, she stopped again and glanced back over her shoulder. "Neil?"

"Yeah?"

"I know it's dumb, but the next time you see Sean, could you ... could you tell him I said goodbye, and that I'll miss him?"

Her tone was so imploring, so sincere. "No problem, Lora. I'll tell him."

She nodded, then hurried the rest of the way to the stairwell.

I stood where I was until I finished the mathematics in my head. Yes, I was sure of it.

Last Thursday had been the last night of the full moon.

Shaken, my thoughts racing, I headed back to my seat in the Green Room.

What exactly had gone *wrong*? Hypnosis alone could not be blamed for the changes in Mark, of that I was positive. For the last two days, I'd been able to keep him under a watchful eye, and not once had he hypnotized himself or taken on the persona of Sean Mallory. And besides, why hadn't *I* been affected? After all, I *started* the whole thing with my assumption of Alistaire Bachman. I was not so egocentric to believe that I possessed some phenomenal willpower that dwarfed that of other men. So what was the difference?

Because of our mutually cluttered schedules, I had no idea when I'd get a chance to talk to Alex, but I would've felt infinitely better if I could have shared my concerns with someone. Maybe Mike Dalton? Or Kathy? No, I didn't want to scare them into thinking that doing *Alistaire* was dangerous. Wouldn't Peter just love *that*?

What *could* be done for Mark? University counseling or student support groups seemed out of the question, even if he agreed to them, which seemed highly unlikely. And I wouldn't even begin to know how to explain his condition to someone.

So your friend is exhibiting changes in his personality?

Yes, ma'am.

And these changes occurred after he began playing the role of a werewolf?

Well, yes, ma'am. I mean, the werewolf part doesn't really matter, I suppose. It's the personality of the man *that we focused on.*

I see. So your friend now believes that he is, in fact, this man who transforms into a wolf.

Well, no, ma'am, not exactly. He knows *that Sean is a character. Not once has he ever said, "I am Sean Mallory." It's just that ...*

I sighed inwardly and shook my head. Oh yes, I could see just where a conversation like *that* would lead. They'd probably throw the straitjacket on *me*.

So what the hell was I supposed to *do*?

*   *   *

Mark met me later that evening after I finished a finals

cram session and we grabbed a bite to eat — I bought, of course. The dinner was long, the conversation was short, and we ended up walking back to my car around eleven-thirty that night.

"... my first priority is getting the university paid so I can get my things out of storage," he was saying in a tired voice. He sighed heavily, wearily. "My mom's pickin' me up tomorrow night."

Part of me, an admittedly *selfish* part, almost asked about what would happen to our comic idea, but good taste held me back. I asked instead, "You'll stay in touch, I hope?"

"Of course I will. Remind me to give you her address and phone number before—"

Mark stopped short as a beer bottle suddenly flew past his head. We turned together.

"What the fuck—!" he spat.

"Hey, Marky," came a deep voice. "Long time, no see."

A half-a-dozen guys stepped out of the shadows of one of the buildings. *I* didn't recognize any of them, but they apparently knew Mark. They sauntered over toward us.

"Mark?"

"Shut up, Neil," he blurted shortly.

The six guys moved closer and closer, slowly spreading out to ring around us. Under the hazy campus lights, with the fatigue of another long day resting on my shoulders like a heavy overcoat, the whole situation reeked of *unreality*. I found it difficult to think clearly, to absorb the connotations of these strangers' actions, but my gut was screaming all sorts of warnings to get the hell out of there.

"What's the matter, Marky-Mark?" asked the one who had spoken before, a tall, square-shouldered, Hispanic guy. "You don't look too happy to see me."

"I'm *not*," Mark said. "I *told* you I'd take care of you.

What're you—"

"Deadline was *two weeks* ago, Marky," spat another guy with a blond flat top, his tone a great deal more venomous than his companion's.

An ugly picture was painting itself: Mark in desperate need of money, up to his ass in debt. Maybe his pride is too much, maybe he thinks asking me for a place to stay is the limit. So he goes elsewhere for money. Loan sharks? Drug runners? Did I really want to know? To be honest and fair, *no*, I didn't. I just wanted to get Mark and myself away in one piece.

I wiped my clammy palms against my jeans. I couldn't recall the last knock-down, drag-out fight I'd been in, but I knew that I'd *never* faced three-to-one odds before. My heart pounded hard against my ribs as I tried desperately to think of a way out of this mess.

"Uh, listen—" I started.

"Shut your mouth," Flat Top growled. "We're busy with your friend here." He stormed toward Mark. "I don't have time for excuses, asshole. Do you have our money or *not*?" When Mark said nothing, Flat Top rumbled through lazy lips, "You're in for a world of hurt, anyway, you little prick. I wouldn't push your fuckin' luck!" He jabbed his finger into Mark's chest so hard it made an audible, hollow thump.

"Look ..." I tried again. I wasn't sure what I was going to say, and I'll never know, because Square Shoulders zeroed in on me.

"Hey, fuckhead, we said we weren't talking to you!" He punctuated his statement with his own stern finger against my chest.

I clamped my mouth shut. Where the fuck were the campus police when you needed them?!

"So, Marky," Flat Top continued, "what's it gonna be?

What's your answer?"

Mark looked him straight in the eye, and even in my cloud of fear, I couldn't miss the accent as he replied, "I'll tell ye what, lad. Why don't ye go fuck yerself?"

For a second, Flat Top's face turned so red that even in the dim light it looked like his head might explode. Everything froze — no sound or movement from anyone or anything, not even the air. Then Flat Top released what sounded like a bark and hit Mark in the stomach with everything he had.

Mark wheezed as his breath left and collapsed in a heap on the ground. Before I could react, Square Shoulders struck me across the cheek, knocking me off balance. I stumbled back, then slipped off the sidewalk and fell onto the grass.

I shook my head, trying to reorient myself. This wasn't a case of bullies picking on the weak — Mark had stepped over the line, and we were in *serious danger*! I heard a *whack* and a groan. From the corner of my eye I saw Flat Top, cursing about money and kicking Mark as he tried to get up. Square Shoulders was standing over me.

"Get up, fuckhead," he rumbled.

I lay on the ground before him, my head ringing, helpless prey before the predator.

helpless prey before the predator

A change washed over me. A cold rush of power flooded my mind, my heart, and my soul.

helpless prey before the predator

I locked my full focus on Square Shoulders, on his spiteful, mean-spirited face, on the sound of his racing heartbeat, on the reek of beer on his breath.

helpless prey before the predator

My head cleared instantly, and I rose to my feet.

helpless prey

Square Shoulders grinned. "That's it, fuckhead. Up for more." He pulled back his fist ...

before the predator

... and swung. His blow landed in the same place as before. My head reeled, I rocked back on my heels ...

... but I didn't fall.

Square Shoulders blinked and swung again. My hand flashed up and locked onto his wrist, and at the same time I stepped back and to the side. He stumbled as the momentum of his swipe carried him past me. I held onto his wrist, pulled him around, and punched him in the jaw. There was an audible *crack* as the bone split, and an odd, sort of grinding, crunchy sound as a few of his teeth broke. Square Shoulders lurched to the side, then fell.

"Holy shit!" someone yelled.

I turned and leaped, tackling another one of them before he could evade me. I felt nothing but strength and confidence now. They wanted a fight — they had one!

I slammed my target's head into the sidewalk once, rendering him abruptly harmless. Another one jumped on my back, but I shrugged him off as if he weighed nothing, as if he *were* nothing.

A fearsome bellow cut the night, and I glanced over to see Mark tearing into Flat Top, his teeth bared, his hands locking around the thumbbreaker's throat.

Good. They were brutes who sought to terrorize those weaker than themselves. They deserved no quarter.

Another body collided with me, and this time I was knocked from my feet, but I rolled easily enough and ended up on top of my assailant. At the last instant I spotted the switchblade in his hand and blocked it bare inches from my face.

"You want my blood?" I demanded. "Do you? *Do you want my blood?*"

His eyes widened in sheer horror. I smiled, opened my mouth, and leaned over him ...

A cry from Mark drew my attention. He had also been attacked with a blade, but had not been so successful in defending himself. Even as he backhanded his opponent, I saw, and smelled, the blood running down his side.

At this point our enemies decided they'd had enough. They ran, staggered, stumbled, and, in Flat Top's case, crawled away. I thought for a moment of chasing after them, but as it became clear that the danger had passed, I felt my sudden charge of strength starting to fade. I hurried to Mark's side. He sat on his heels on the ground, his body doubled over, his hand gripping his side, his forehead against the grass.

"Mark?" I asked. "You all right?"

"They're gone?" he grunted.

"Yeah, they're gone."

"Alistaire," he said, "help me up."

I stared at him for a beat, then decided not to correct him as I helped him to his feet.

The campus police never did show up.

*   *   *

Less than twenty-four hours later, as I escorted Mark to the front gate of my apartment complex, the events of the previous night were already a blur to me. Had I been asked about them then, I could not have described them as I have now. Like my incident with Alicia, it had clouded over in my mind. All I remembered was being surrounded and asked for money, a fight of some sort, and Mark's cut, which luckily turned out to be more painful than lethal, a surface cut about six inches across but not even a quarter-inch deep. Of our assailants I could recall only two things: The faces of Square

Shoulders and Flat Top.

Mark's stride was a little stiff, but it wasn't that noticeable if you didn't know to look for it. What concerned me more than anything else was that slight touch of an Irish dialect that still infused his voice.

It was raining as Mark and I walked in silence to where his mother waited. He had only a backpack with a few clothes crammed inside — all his other possessions belonged to the university for now.

We stopped a few yards from his mother's car.

"I've gotta be goin' now," he said.

I looked up at him, my heart heavy. "Can I ask you a question?"

"Yes."

"Am I speaking to Mark now, or Sean?"

He paused. "I don't rightly know. A little of both, I suppose."

I nodded.

"I know I told ye I'd give ye my mother's address and phone number. I ... I think I'd rather not, if ye don't mind. It's nothing personal, of course. I just need to isolate myself for a while. I'll get in touch with ye when I feel I can."

"I understand." Pause. "Mark ... please ... get some help."

He looked at the ground. "I think I will."

I swallowed against the lump rising in my throat and the growing crack in my voice. "I'm sorry ... I'm sorry if I've somehow *done* this to you."

"Ye haven't done anything, Ali— Neil," he told me flatly. "Believe that. No matter what's happened to me, it's much larger than anything ye could have done with hypnosis. I can feel that much in my bones."

I didn't know whether or not he was right, but it felt good to hear it, anyway.

"Goodbye, Mark," I said. "I'll miss you. Good luck."

He shifted his backpack to his other shoulder and headed for the car.

"Mark," I called after him.

He stopped and looked back.

"Lora said to tell ... she said to tell you goodbye, and that she would miss you, too."

He smiled. "That's a nice gesture, Neil, but I think we both know whom that message was *really* for, don't we, lad?"

I said nothing.

Mark waved, climbed into the car, and was driven away.

REVELATIONS

SIXTEEN

"Spending time as Alistaire has really had an influence on me," I commented to Kathy after the hostess seated us and walked away. The scent of food, sounds of conversation on all sides, heat from the kitchen, cold from the over-taxed air conditioners ... "I swear my senses haven't been this sharp my whole life."

Kathy smiled and nodded, almost knowingly.

After finals, two weeks passed before the right opportunity for Kathy and me to go on our first date arrived. Peter was otherwise occupied, giving us privacy but also bringing her curfew down by one hour. Even without any knowledge of hypnosis or other pagan activities, Karl Schaumburg reigned in his strict views not one iota. An older man had asked his little girl out to dinner, and her brother would not be in attendance? Somehow he thought that bringing her in at eleven instead of midnight would somehow keep "things" from happening.

At one point during our dinner, Kathy swallowed her bite of hamburger, wiped her mouth with her napkin, and asked, "Why do you think Alistaire has to suffer?"

"I'm sorry?" I was thrown off-guard by the sudden topic. "What do you mean?"

"He's such a noble person," she elaborated, "such a majestic, regal soul. He says that God chose him to carry out

His will. But why *him*? Why does *he* have to suffer? His mission strikes me as far more of a curse than a blessing."

"Well, uh," I stammered, "from what I know about Alistaire, he's just accepted it as something he shouldn't question. A matter of faith, or maybe just *Divine Fate*."

"But why is *that* his fate?" she pleaded, her concern touching and alarming at the same time.

I shrugged, uncomfortable and unable to think of any response other than, "He says it isn't his place to question God, Kathy."

She hesitated, then nodded, accepting my statement without further comment. Absently, she seized her straw behind her first and middle fingers and punched repeatedly at the ice in her glass.

I was tempted to reiterate the fact that Alistaire wasn't a real person, but I knew Kathy was intelligent enough to already understand that.

"Was he close to his family?"

At least, I *thought* she understood it ...

"As close as anyone was at the time, I guess. He says blood relations were held in much more 'formal regard' back when he was mortal. His parents died when he was a teenager. It's sad, but he doesn't have very many memories of them."

"My parents were divorced before I was ten. It was a pretty rough court battle. The only reason my father won custody was because of his money, and he made it look like my mother was an alcoholic."

"I take it that was a lie?"

Kathy shrugged. "Not anymore. But she wasn't as bad *before* the estrangement. Go figure."

I thought for a moment, debating whether or not to push forward into an area that was almost certainly none of my business. Finally I said, "You're eighteen years old, Kathy.

You're going to be a college Sophomore. Why do you and Peter let your father keep such a tight hold on you?"

"It's that old law of 'As long as you live under my roof' ... I don't know. I can't afford to move out on my own, much less continue college without help. If I ever bucked his system too hard, he'd cut me off."

"How does Peter feel about the situation?"

"Oh, he claims to hate it as much as I do, but he's also more than happy to play the favored child. I may not talk back as much as I'd like to, but I'm not the 'Yes-Man' that Peter is."

"I'm sorry. Too bad Alistaire's money is locked away in another world. I'm sure he'd be more than happy to pay for your school and housing."

Kathy stared into my eyes, almost as if she were searching for something. She drew a breath, and I saw that her bottom lip was quivering. Before she could speak, however, I glanced over her shoulder, and my mind tried to grasp what I was seeing.

"Neil?" Kathy whispered. "What's wrong?"

I stood and stepped across the bar area toward the television. On the screen, in a caption to the right of a news anchorwoman was a double picture of Flat Top and Square Shoulders.

"Excuse me," I said to the bartender. "Could you turn up the volume on the TV, please?"

The bartender shrugged and clicked the remote a couple of times.

"... were found dead this morning, both apparently the victims of a harrowing double-murder near the University of Oklahoma in Norman. The families of the victims ..."

The newswoman's voice-over told of their relatives' oaths that they were model citizens, "good kids," while the screen showed paramedics moving the covered bodies onto the back of a coroner's van with no particular hurry.

"While police investigators are withholding details of the bloody killing, Channel Four News was able to get a brief word from the man who discovered the bodies."

The scene changed to a janitor that I immediately recognized from the Fine Arts Center. The sallow-faced custodian strode quickly from one building to another while reporters thrust microphones in his face, demanding to know everything he'd seen that morning. His only intelligible response was, "Let's just say that I fought in Korea, and I ain't *never* seen nothin' like it!"

The picture cut back to the newsroom, and the anchor began her segue into the weather.

"What is it?" Kathy asked from my side. "Do you know those guys?"

"I had a ... run-in with them," I told her as I tried, unsuccessfully, to recall the exact details of that night before Mark's departure. "Maybe they finally loaned money to the wrong people." Kathy looked confused at that. I waved it away. "Never mind. It's nothing to worry about." I glanced at a clock over the bar. "It's getting close to your curfew. I'd better get you home."

Nudging her away, I turned my back to the television.

SEVENTEEN

I tried, I really *tried*, not to think about the murders of Flat Top and Square Shoulders. They were a couple of assholes who got what was probably coming to them, and that was that.

At least, I *wanted* "that" to be "that." But as the days passed and the news refused to die, I could no longer push it out of my mind.

The loan sharks, assuming that's what they really had been all along, had been *torn apart*. All the papers and every hour of televised news hammered the information into the population's collective mind over and over ...

Torn apart
as if by
an animal

If only Mark had given me his mother's number, I might've been able to alleviate my concerns with a simple phone call. Unfortunately, long-distance information proved useless, so I just walked around helplessly with the suspicions and qualms growing in my gut.

By the fourth evening, I could no longer keep everything to myself. I needed, *desperately*, to talk to someone. Alex Monroe had gone home for the summer, so, after much soul-searching, I decided that Kathy and Mike were the way to go.

*   *   *

They arrived at my apartment at about the same time, Kathy predictably with Peter in tow. I kept trying to think of a way to breach the subject, but I just didn't feel comfortable with Peter around. My vague behavior obviously confused everyone, but they seemed content to wait for me. Finally, unable to think of a more tactful way around it, I suggested that Peter run down to the vending machines for a Coke.

Clueless, he said, "No, thanks."

"Peter," Kathy explained as if to a child, "I think Neil wants to have a private conversation with Mike and me."

"So?" he smiled. "I'm family, right?"

"Peter," I snapped, "get lost."

Even before my mouth closed, I regretted it. Peter went rigid.

"Peter—" Kathy soothed, but he was already walking stiffly out the front door. I expected him to slam it behind him, but instead he pulled it gently shut.

"Sorry," I mumbled.

Kathy sighed. "It's all right. He's going to have to get it through his head sooner or later that we are *not siamese twins*."

"I still shouldn't have said it." One of the things I was growing to love about her was that she hated to hurt anyone's feelings at any time for any reason. "I'll apologize to him later, okay?"

"Okay." She smiled and moved closer to me.

"What did you want to talk to us about?" Mike asked.

I took a deep breath. I had them to myself now, so I no longer had any excuse for stalling.

"I ... I, uh, think I might know something about ... those murders that took place by the school."

Two pairs of eyebrows shot up. Kathy stammered, "The

animal killings?"

"Uh, yeah, the 'animal killings.' That's right."

Mike followed right up with, "What *exactly* might you know about them?"

"Well—"

"That's right!" Kathy burst suddenly. "At the restaurant, that first night, you said you knew them."

"And I told you I had a run-in with them."

"Yes." She was looking decidedly nervous now, and Mike wasn't exactly at ease himself.

"Do you remember when I told you about Mark, the guy I was doing the Alistaire comic book with?"

They both nodded.

Here goes nothing ...

I spilled my guts. I told them everything I knew, from Mark's financial problems — including what Alistaire witnessed at the 7-11 — to his behavior related to Sean Mallory, and finally to what I could remember of the night involving the recently deceased.

"And so," Mike concluded for me, "you think your friend might have come back and killed these loan sharks."

I nodded. "I'm sorry to say that's what I'm starting to wonder."

"That's incredible," Kathy said.

"Yes," Mike agreed, "but it doesn't necessarily make sense."

"How so?" I asked. Believe me, I would have *loved* for Mike to prove me absolutely wrong.

"First of all, if the news is even *half* accurate, these men were ripped to *shreds*. Even if Mark did come back, how could he do it?"

"I admit, under *normal* circumstances, I'd be afraid for *his* life in a Round Two. But if he's gone all the way with this Sean thing ..."

"And if Sean turned into a wolf—"

Mike shook his head adamantly. "Kathy, that still doesn't explain it. Even if he *believed* he transformed into a werewolf, that doesn't change reality. I understand those men really were mauled. Even if we assume his psychosis gave him extra strength, it doesn't track."

"But who *else* could have done it?" I pushed back. "*Real* animals wouldn't make sense, and I'd guess it's safe to assume none of their other clients had *lycanthropy* on the mind."

Mike considered me for a moment. "Neil, have *you* had any ... uh, *difficulties* from doing Alistaire?"

"None," I answered with confidence. "That's one of the reasons I didn't jump on this problem with Mark right off the bat. It was all so *harmless* for me, I couldn't imagine why it would affect him any differently."

"Maybe that's something," Kathy perked. "Why don't you go into Alistaire and we'll ask him what Sean's been up to lately?"

Mike and I exchanged a subtly baffled look. "Kathy, neither Alistaire nor Sean are real, so—"

"I know what Neil's explained to us, Mike. We've all heard it several times now, and it's nice of you to remind us." She wasn't being sarcastic, but spoke as if *we* were the ones who weren't getting it. "But have you ever stopped to wonder, just for a minute, Neil, if maybe there's *more* to Alistaire than you believe?"

"No," I told her, ignoring the inner flinch her observation caused. "I haven't. Alistaire is nothing but a character." I stiffened my posture, kept myself from blinking, and lowered my voice a half-step. "As you can see, Ms. Schaumburg, I can affect him whenever I want."

Kathy actually giggled at that, and even Mike smiled in spite of himself. "Sorry, Neil, but that's not quite the same."

Pushing away a hint of irritation, I said, "All right, watch this." After all the practice I'd had, I figured that at least a partial merging would be no problem. Maybe if she saw that I could conjure him up and send him away at any moment that would convince ...

Nothing happened. Not even a twitch from Alistaire.

"Watch what?" she asked.

My face flushed as I realized the awkward position I'd just put myself in. They sat there, expectant. I reached inward again, but for some reason, my Alistaire persona was nowhere in sight.

"Nothing," I muttered, confused and embarrassed. "Besides, we aren't here to debate over *Alistaire*. I'm seriously wondering if I should go to the police about Mark, and I was hoping for both of your ... "

I trailed off as a low creak crept through the apartment. Kathy couldn't see from where she was, but Mike and I both regarded the slowly swinging front door. It drifted all the way open ... revealing no one, just the empty landing.

"Peter must not have closed the door all the way when he left," Mike observed.

"Oh," Kathy whispered, her face falling pale.

"Kathy?"

"Oh, no." She rushed through the door and out onto the landing, leaning over the railing and craning her neck toward the parking lot.

"What's that all about?" I asked. Mike shrugged.

Slowly, as if feeling sick, Kathy marched back into the apartment. She looked like she wanted to cry.

"Kathy?" I went to her, gently putting my hands on her shoulders. "Are you all right? What's wrong?"

"The car," she answered in a low voice.

" 'The car?' " Mike echoed.

"It's gone. *Peter's* gone."

*   *   *

I drove around the corner and coasted until we reached Kathy's house, then parked along the curb. Sure enough, their car sat in the driveway.

"So, how long do you figure he was listening to us?" I fumed. She was obviously upset, and objectively I knew this could cause trouble with her militant father, but I couldn't get past the *offense* of Peter's eavesdropping on us.

Kathy's breathing came quickly. She jumped when the porch light went on. "I'm afraid it was long enough," she whispered.

I followed her gaze.

Karl Schaumburg stormed out of the house. Peter lagged a few steps behind him, his eyes downcast, possibly already feeling guilty about what he'd done.

"Get out of that car, Katherine," he commanded in a German accent far thicker than I'd ever heard from my vampire friend.

Kathy did as she was told, and I followed suit.

"Vater, what—" she began, but he lifted his rigid hand to cut her off.

"Heil, Hitler," I muttered to myself.

Karl Schaumburg really was the late Fuehrer's picturesque Aryan. Fair skin, broad shoulders, stern jaw, crystal blue eyes, flaxen hair cut military short. How such a sweet girl had come from such an uptight asshole was beyond me. Up until now, I'd managed to observe him only from a distance, but things were about to get up close and personal.

"Peter tells me that this young man has been luring you into serious trouble, with *murderers* and games of *mesmerism*. Is this true?" he demanded.

"No!" she exclaimed. She then quickly lowered her

voice and her gaze and continued, "I mean, no, sir."

"Then you are saying your brother has *lied* to me?"

"Well, no ..."

I tried to help out. "Um, Mr. Schaumburg—"

His head snapped toward me so sharply that his neck actually popped. "I am not speaking to you, *Mr. Carpenter*. I am speaking to my daughter." The tyrant shifted his attention back to her and barked, "Well? *Answer*."

Kathy wavered as she admitted, "Neil *thinks* that he *might* have some information about the men that were killed. And he *has* shown some of us a little of what he knows about hypnotism.   But it's nothing they don't teach you in Psychology at school—!"

"And that is exactly why I kept you *out* of that class, young lady!" His face was no longer pale, but beet red. "And so now he has played these mind games and people have been *slaughtered*."

Kathy stared at Peter accusingly. "You ran home to tell him, without even knowing what—"

"Don't you dare try to turn this around against your brother, Katherine!" her father bellowed. "Peter did right in telling me about this appalling new boyfriend of yours."

My temper was getting shorter by the second. "Look, Mr. Schaumburg—"

"*I said I am speaking to my daughter*.   I will have nothing to do with you, and from now on, neither will *she*."

"Vater!" Kathy cried. "You can't—"

He seized her fiercely by the shoulder and shoved her toward the house. "Go inside and wait for me!"

Like a good little soldier, Peter guided Kathy into the house. She looked back at me the whole way, tears in her eyes but not saying a word.

"Stay *away*, Mr. Carpenter," Karl Schaumburg said to me, and there was no mistaking that his words danced the fine line between warning and threat. "Stay away from my daughter and my son. I don't know how *your* parents raised you, but it is clear how you have turned out. Once I have dealt with my children, I believe I will inform the *authorities* of your little practices. And if you ever come near my children again, I will take the law into my *own* hands. *Do I make myself clear?*"

I said nothing. I was trembling with such rage that I didn't trust myself to speak.

Karl Schaumburg did an about-face and marched his militant ass back into the house, ready to do God only knew *what* to someone I cared about a great deal. But what could I do?

I peeled rubber away from the curb, down the street, and around the next corner. I was furious and upset, my emotions in such chaos that I could barely see straight. After driving out of the neighborhood I slammed on the brakes and leaped from the car. My furor built and built until I could no longer contain it, and I threw my head back and screamed at the top of my lungs until my throat hurt.

I couldn't take this. I couldn't stand to feel so helpless, so powerless. I had to do something. But what?

Then I knew.

I could become someone who *could* do something. Someone who was *never* helpless, *never* powerless.

Then my mind was lost in a shroud of ivory mist.

EIGHTEEN

I reached up to scratch my side.

That's weird, some slowly awakening part of my mind noted. I usually wear a T-shirt to bed, but it felt like I was wearing *silk*.

I opened my eyes.

I *was* wearing silk, my gold silk shirt.

I sat upright. I was in my apartment, in bed. What was I doing in bed in my gold silk shirt and black slacks? The last thing I remembered ...

... was screaming into the night ...

... and an ivory mist.

My brain kicked into overdrive, or at least it tried to. What had happened last night? Where had I gone? What had I done? When did I change clothes? I didn't remember coming home, but here I was. How?

I leaped to my feet and paced back and forth, frantically trying to clear my head. I took off my silk shirt and tossed it unceremoniously onto the back of my chair. I knew that Alistaire wouldn't approve, but ...

Damn it, what fucking difference did it make what Alistaire *thought?!*

I stopped pacing. Oh, man, I was losing it.

I collapsed onto my bed, bracing my elbows on my knees and cradling my head in my hands. *Think*. I had to *think*.

I'd pulled the car over, jumped out, then ... *damn* it! I couldn't *remember*!

At least, I couldn't remember any *actions*, any facts. I did, however, recall a sensation, a feeling of power. It was like deja vu, in a way. It had been *strength*, like ...

Like the night with Flat Top and Square Shoulders.

Oh, my God.

It wasn't *Mark* I needed to worry about. It was *me*.

It had gotten away from me. Just like Mark. Alex Monroe was right — I had been playing games with Pandora's Box, and God only knew what the consequences would be. Insanity? Unfortunately, that sounded like a distinct possibility. I mean, a sane person would probably remember how he got home and into someone else's clothes.

There I went again. Those weren't *Alistaire's* clothes, they were *mine*.

What if I *killed them?*

Fighting a wave of nausea, I grabbed the phone. I needed Kathy.

I dialed her number and cupped the receiver with my palm. If her father or Peter picked up the line, I'd have to hang up.

It didn't matter. There was no answer.

I left the confines of my room and spread my pacing across the entire apartment. Did I do it? When exactly did the murders take place? Where had I been, could I remember *that*?

And what in God's name had I done *last* night?

I decided to call Mike Dalton. Maybe talking to *him* would calm me down. Maybe he might happen to know where Kathy was, have some idea of how I could get a hold of her.

"Hello?"

"Mike. It's Neil."

There was a pause.

"Mike?"

"Neil, have you seen the news?"

"Uh, no. I just got up." I began to feel cold inside. "Why?"

"I think you'd better see for yourself. Turn on channel five right now."

I snatched up the TV remote.

It was the lunch-hour news. The scene was almost exactly like the one I'd first seen in the restaurant, with two bodies being loaded onto a meat wagon.

"Is this a recap of the Norman murders?"

"Keep watching."

The story continued to sound like a repeat of the one before, until two faces appeared on the screen, and they didn't belong to Flat Top and Square Shoulders.

"Dean Leitner and Susan Tate were students at the University of Oklahoma, where just a few days ago ..."

I dropped the phone.

"Neil?" drifted Mike's voice.

I fell forward, trying to vomit but only heaving.

Oh, God, it was *me, I did it, oh, God*

"Neil? Neil!"

My hand felt numb as it closed on the phone, but then my fingers gripped it so tightly I'm surprised it didn't shatter. My breath shuddered through my aching chest.

"Mike," I asked, overriding his next call and fighting to keep the tremor out of my voice, "have you heard from Kathy today?"

"Um, no. I haven't talked to her since you guys left last night. What happened to Peter? And what happened to *you* just now?"

"Peter went home. He listened in on us, told their Dad

what he heard, and all about how the hypnotic games might have affected Mark. Got Kathy in a lot of trouble."

"That little jerk."

"Mike, listen to me ..." It almost came out with tears.

Easy, Neil, I thought. *You can't afford to freak out just yet.*

"Mike, listen," I repeated, forcing a pseudo-calm back into my voice. "I need your help. Kathy's dad's forbidden her to see me, but I've *got* to talk to her, to both of you. They're not home right now, but can you call in a little while for me? See if there's any way to get her out of there? Maybe we can meet at your place or something. Please."

He waited a second before answering. I guessed that my attempt to hide my anxiety hadn't worked. "Sure," he said finally. "I'll start calling every half-hour or so, let you know when I get a hold of her. Are you at home right now?"

"Yeah."

"All right, I'll be in touch then." A beat. "Neil, are you okay?"

"Fine," I lied. "But I *need* to talk. I'll be waiting to hear from you."

I hung up, then just sat there and tried not to cry.

*   *   *

Two-and-a-half torturous hours later, the phone rang. I expected it to be, *prayed* that it would be Mike with news about Kathy. Instead, I was blessedly shocked to find Kathy herself on the line.

"Kathy!" I cried, and the tears I'd long been fighting back found their way to the surface.

"Neil," she whispered, "are you all right?"

"No," I admitted, running a shaking hand through my hair. "Did Mike get in touch with you? I tried to call earlier but there was no answer."

"I know. My father unplugged the phone. He got a page a little while ago and had to run to the office. As soon as he left I plugged it back in and it was already ringing. I thought it might be you, but it was Mike. He told me to call while I had the chance."

"Why are you whispering?"

"Peter's here. He feels guilty about what he did last night, so I don't *think* he would tell, but I'm not taking any chances."

"I understand." I breathed deeply. "Have you heard the news?"

"About Dean and Susan? Yes. Why would Sean—"

"Kathy ..." Another deep breath. "... I think *I* might have done it."

"What?!" she blurted, heedless of her raised voice.

"I don't remember anything about last night, Kathy," I confessed. "After your father flipped out, I left your house, stopped a little ways down the road ... and then I woke up in bed around noon, and I was wearing Alistaire's clothes."

"Oh." Her voice now sounded frighteningly small.

"I know I shouldn't be dropping this in your lap. I'm sorry, but I need to talk to someone. I'm losing myself, Kathy. I'm going *fucking insane*."

I really started breaking down at that point. Only her next words kept me focused.

"Neil, listen to me. Are you still at home?"

"Y-yeah."

"I'm coming over."

"Kathy, I don't know if—"

"Shh! Not another word. I'm coming over."

I knew that I should argue with her, try to convince her that it wasn't a good idea to antagonize her father any further, but my fear made me weak.

"All right," I said. "But I don't want to meet here. I—I've just got to get out of here. Mike's. Meet me at Mike's."

"Okay. I'll call to let him know we're coming. Do you want me to call anyone else? It sounds like you could use—"

"No! Please. Just you, and Mike."

"Okay. I'll see you soon. Hold on, Neil. Believe me, you'll be all right."

*   *   *

I got to Mike's ahead of her. He escorted me to his bedroom with as few words to his parents as possible. He asked no questions, for which I was thankful.

Fifteen minutes later, Kathy arrived. As soon as she walked into his room, I melted into her arms. Mike closed the door and sat down in a chair. After a minute of close contact, Kathy guided me to the bed.

"Did you get away all right?" I asked.

She nodded. "I waited until Peter was in the bathroom, then took the car keys and made a break for it. My father still wasn't home when I left."

"There'll be hell to pay," I told her.

"I don't care about that right now." She took my face in her hands. "Neil, listen to me, and listen closely. There is *no way* that you could be responsible for what happened to Dean and Susan."

"What?" Mike exclaimed, coming to full attention in a heartbeat. Kathy waved him away without breaking her gaze from me.

"You don't understand, Kathy," I told her. "Things are coming apart." I pulled away from her, this time running both hands through my hair to the back of my neck, my eyes shut tight. "All this time, I've been worried about Mark, when the truth was *Alistaire* was getting away from *me*."

"What about everything you told us about hypnosis," Mike tried, "about how you were always in control of—"

I shook my head. "This has nothing to do with hypnosis anymore." I told him about my blackout the night before, and then waking up in different clothes. "I wasn't hypnotized. I think I'm just losing touch with reality. I need serious help." I couldn't escape the image of Mark, speaking in that Irish accent, right before he left with his mother. How far away was *I* from that kind of behavior? Or, in light of it all, how much *worse* was I already?

"Neil," Kathy said, "we'll talk about Alistaire in a minute. For now let's focus on whether or not you killed Susan and Dean."

I covered my face and stifled a sob, but I nodded.

"First of all, did you find any blood on yourself?"

"What ... uh, no." I hadn't thought about any of the details, just the terror that I was responsible.

"According to the news, they were brutally, *savagely* murdered. Just like the other two. How could you have done that without getting a drop of blood on you?"

"I ... no, that still doesn't mean anything. If I thought I was Alistaire, then I guess I would have drank—"

"Drank the blood of two people, without getting *covered* in gore?" she demanded. "That's not possible, Neil. But it does bring me to my next point. You basically believe that you became Alistaire last night. Now whether or not Alistaire is real, I think we've come to know him pretty well. You've made an absolute case study of him. Do you really think that Alistaire Bachman, God-chosen protector of mankind and leader of the Triumvirate, would have murdered two obnoxious but otherwise innocent human beings?"

I was speechless, but Mike answered her for me. "No,"

he said with confidence, "he wouldn't."

"Of course he wouldn't," Kathy said. "Whoever is doing it, it can't be Alistaire."

"Well ..." As contradictory as it might sound, I almost felt as if I had to defend my *guilt* at this point. "What if I didn't exactly become Alistaire himself. Maybe I just—"

Kathy firmly shook her head. "No, Neil. I suppose that could have happened along the way, but things are too set now. You became Alistaire, Neil. That's all there is to it."

"Um, listen, guys," Mike said uneasily. "I don't want to sound too harsh, Neil, but I think Kathy's making this a little too clean cut. I don't want to believe that you had anything to do with the murders, Neil, but I think we can't get away from the fact that you *do* need some kind of help. The fact that you can still recognize that there's a problem is a good sign, but let's not lose touch with the fact that Alistaire Bachman is *still* just a fictitious character."

Kathy was shaking her head again. "No, Mike. I'm afraid you don't understand. Right or wrong, for better or worse, for whatever reason, Alistaire is *real*."

I felt too numb to do anything but watch their exchange. I kept waiting for some still-sane part of me to speak up, but it never did. My mind was so hazy I found it difficult to think.

"Kathy," Mike said, and his tone was on the edge of hostility, "Neil doesn't need to hear that sort of garbage right now. Alistaire *does not exist*."

Almost with pity, Kathy smiled at him, then at me, then straight ahead. "Look," she told us with a brief gesture.

Mike and I turned to face his dresser.

My eyes widened in shock, and what was left of my consciousness reeled.

Mike's breath caught audibly in his throat as he stammered, "Jesus Christ!"

Kathy just smiled and nodded knowingly.

In the dresser mirror, Kathy and Mike were reflected plain as day, just as they should have been. The image of myself, however, was faded, ghostly, semi-transparent, like when facing a plain glass window with the lights on inside and the sheer darkness of night outside.

I was only casting half a reflection.

My mind overloaded. I passed out.

NINETEEN

"Neil?" Mike asked, his voice still saturated with the horror of what he'd seen in the mirror. He was terrified, but our friendship was strong enough to concern him when I suddenly slumped almost to the point of falling off the bed.

Kathy reached out a hand to steady me, once again more privy to what was happening than seemed possible. "Easy," she whispered.

Alistaire reached up to pat her hand. *"I'm fine now. Thank you."*

"Oh, Jesus," Mike mumbled and stepped back as Alistaire straightened up and stretched.

The German vampire glanced at him for a moment, then returned his attention to the German mortal. *"How did you know?"* he asked.

She shrugged. "Woman's intuition."

Alistaire wasn't satisfied with that. *"This must seem quite impossible to you. Take Michael here, for instance. His is the more expected of the two reactions, you must admit."*

"I know," she agreed. "I guess I'm just more open-minded than most people."

Alistaire smiled, then laughed at that.

"Okay," Mike said, finally getting a grip on himself. "Okay. Could ... could one of you ... tell me *exactly* what's happening here?"

Alistaire nodded. *"That seems fair enough. I'll illuminate things for you as best I can — there's Divine Intervention here that even I do not fully comprehend."*

He stood, walking slowly toward Mike's bedroom window, his hands clasped casually behind his back. Even though the window faced the east, the still-bright sky was a little overwhelming for him, and he quickly turned away. If not for my residual presence, he knew that he wouldn't even be conscious at this time of day.

"How 'exactly' our two worlds are related to one another — the mechanics of that relationship — is a mystery to me. The first night that I felt Neil Carpenter's essence call upon me, I knew that something extraordinary was taking place. The hypnotic sessions helped bridge the rift between us, but there was always something more involved. Perhaps, in some bizarre fashion, he and I are kindred souls. I can only guess, and have faith." He sat on the edge of the bed and addressed them directly. *"You, Michael, argued that I am fictitious, that I do not exist. Are you familiar with the philosopher Descartes?"* Mike glanced at Kathy, then shook his head. *"While he is renowned for his philosophical arguments to prove the existence of G-God, he is perhaps most famous for this singular quote: 'Cogito, ergo sum' — 'I think, therefore I am.'"* He spread his arms without a hint of dramatic flare, then continued, *"Comparatively, my world is imbued, permeated with the supernatural. Yours was virgin substance until recently. The fact that I sit here before you can only signify the beginning of a dramatic change in the fabric of your world as you know it. To be frank, you are about to urgently need me."* He paused, collecting his thoughts, then continued, *"The process was a difficult one. In the early stages, as my essence sought to steal itself into Neil's, there were a few*

instances when my control was not firmly established, and Neil's own spirit was too weak, or too unprepared, to handle what was happening. On two occasions, one which involved a night of passion with a dance student from the university and the other the two ruffians recently slaughtered, events almost ran amok. Fortunately, I was able, over time, to infuse myself more sufficiently, and then ..." Again the spread arms, this time even more subdued than before.

Mike breathed out heavily through his mouth, his cheeks puffing out in almost comical exasperation. "Well, I can't deny what I've seen with my own eyes." He gestured with his head toward the dresser mirror. "So, what's next?" Then, with sudden intensity, he added, "And what happens to Neil?"

"I'm afraid we'll have to deal with that question another time. For now, we have pressing business to attend to."

Disoriented, Mike shook his head. "Which is ...?"

"The murders," Kathy answered.

"The murders," Alistaire confirmed. *"As Ms. Schaumburg here admirably argued on my behalf, I assure you, I am* not *responsible for the recent deaths that have plagued the area."*

"Then who is?" Mike demanded.

"I have my suspicions. To confirm them, I must go to the university. Let me simply say that Neil's first thoughts might not have been far off track."

Mike grunted. "You think it *was* Sean."

"Specifically, Mark, *out of Sean's control. After seeing some of Mark's illustrations that he found personally disturbing, Sean, in* my *world, withdrew to Ireland out of a need for soul-searching. I have, therefore, been out of touch with him, and cannot personally confer with him."*

"I'm going with you," Kathy told him.

Alistaire shook his head. *"I would prefer that you didn't. The potential for danger is too great. If Mark has indeed—"*

"Correct me if I'm wrong, Mr. Bachman," Kathy said, her hands on her hips, "but if we can still see even *part* of Neil's reflection in that mirror, that tells me that you have not fully 'arrived' yet. Until then, I think it would be a good idea if you had a little help."

"Katherine—"

Mike chuckled.   "Alistaire, after five-and-a-half centuries of existence, haven't you learned that you can't change a woman's mind once it's been made up?"

Alistaire's eyebrow lifted. *"Indeed."*

"Then it's settled." She stood. "You coming, too, Mike?"

"I ..." He looked at Alistaire, but I strongly suspect that in that moment, he saw only *me*. "I suppose I have to see this thing through. Not exactly your everyday experience we're dealing with here, now is it? I think half of my brain is still running to catch up."

"I should stop by my house first," Kathy said, her tone suggesting that she'd rather stop by a toxic waste site. "My father'll go berserk over this, but at least he won't be calling the police to report me as a runaway."

Alistaire grunted. *"Since you see fit to accompany me, I think it would be only fair for me to join you in your difficult task as well."*

"Do you really think that's a good idea?" Mike asked, rising to his feet. "I mean, you still *look* like Neil, and that's all that Kathy's dad'll see."

"He's right, Alistaire," she admitted. "I don't think your being there will help."

"Oh, I don't know. I can be quite persuasive when I put

my mind to it."

*   *   *

The three of them waited — at Alistaire's understandable request — for the sun to sink below the horizon. While they lingered, Kathy joined him as he sat before the window watching the darkening sky.

"Alistaire?"

"Yes?"

"May I ask you a question?"

"Of course."

"Now that we've established that you weren't at the scene of Dean and Susan's murders, I was wondering ... where *were* you last night?"

In a soft, gentle, totally unexpected display of affection, Alistaire reached over and took her hand in his own. *"I was outside your house,"* he confessed, *"making certain that your Vater made no move to hurt you."*

Kathy smiled, and rested her head on his shoulder.

*   *   *

Alistaire could hear Kathy's racing heart and smell her perspiration as they pulled into the driveway. Her hands were gripping the steering wheel with strength sufficient to render her knuckles bloodless. He again reached over to hold her hand in his own, but the gesture was notably less calming now that her confrontation was imminent.

"Should, uh, should I stay in the car?" Mike asked.

"Yes," she answered quickly. Then, "No ... I don't know. Jesus, this is going to be hard."

"Katherine, maybe it would *be best if you did not accompany me tonight."*

"*No.* I told you I was going to help you, and I'm going to keep my word." Her resolve set, her shoulders taut, she opened the door and got out of the car.

"This will not take as long as she fears," Alistaire told Mike in the backseat as he opened his own door. *"I will allow her a chance to deal with this herself — she deserves no less. But if Mr. Schaumburg persists with his imperious state, then I will have to demonstrate that Neil Carpenter is not the only one knowledgeable in 'games of mesmerism'."*

Mike grunted and grinned. "I'm tempted to go in just to see that."

Kathy was already at the door when Alistaire caught up with her. "I'm surprised," she told him as she inserted her key into the lock. "I expected him to be waiting outside on the porch. He has to be home by now, and regardless of how guilty he may or may not feel, I know Peter would be pretty much incapable of covering for me."

Alistaire said nothing, but waited for her to lead the way.

When she opened the door, he knew immediately that something was awry. The ambience of the house was ... disturbed in some way. A moment later, he smelled the blood.

"Katherine," he snapped sharply, seizing her arm before she could walk inside.

"Wha—?" she got out before he clamped a gentle but firm hand over her mouth.

"Something is wrong," he told her in a low voice. *"Go back and stay with Michael."*

She undoubtedly wanted to protest, but his firm conviction held her in check. She did as he said, and he entered the house alone.

The scent of carnage hung about the air like a thick fog. Most of the lights were out, but his growing vampiric presence more than compensated for the mortal limitations of my vision. With unnatural grace, he moved about the house.

He found Peter in the living room, curled up in a fetal ball, his eyes wide but seeing nothing. At first glance, Alistaire feared that he was dead, but a closer examination revealed that he was merely in deep shock. Whatever had happened here this evening, Peter had evidently witnessed it, and his mind had not been able to handle it.

For the moment, Alistaire abandoned Kathy's brother to search the back rooms. His senses told him even before he reached the study that he'd found the source of the bloody fetor.

The window to the study had exploded inward as the offender leaped bodily through the glass. Karl Schaumburg had tried in vain to defend himself, but his fate had already been decided. His arterial spray had painted a grotesque portrait upon the walls, floor, and ceiling of the room as he'd spun about, perhaps locked arm-in-arm with his assailant.

Alistaire breathed deep, seeking the scent that might identify the man's attacker, but the only smell his olfactory could detect was the sweet aroma of Schaumburg's blood. He then leaned forward to examine the body where it had finally fallen. Schaumburg's guts rested in strings across his lap and legs. His throat was an open cavity, bitten not across the windpipe, but lengthwise from chin to sternum, leaving a fairly shallow but long canyon in his flesh. The tendons of his neck, now visible, were still taut from when he had probably tried to scream.

With a delicate hand, Alistaire reached out and pulled a wispy substance from one of the wounds.

Animal hair.

Returning to the living room, Alistaire considered Peter. They could not afford to linger any further, but neither could the boy be brought along in his current state. And above all else, Alistaire was determined to keep Kathy out of this house.

He picked up the phone, dialed 9-1-1, and set the receiver down off the cradle. The authorities would trace the call and take the proper steps, assuring Peter help and themselves a chance to get away.

Leaving the house, Alistaire opened the car door and slipped into the passenger seat. Kathy was almost delirious with worry.

"What was it?!" she demanded.

Alistaire looked her firmly in the eye. *"Your brother will be fine."*

"But what about—"

"Katherine," he repeated, his timbre unyielding, *"it is imperative that we go to the university* now. *If we do not, it is inevitable that many more people will be brought to harm. Your brother will be fine, but we must leave without delay."*

Kathy held her breath, closed her eyes, and made a leap of faith. "All right."

She backed the car out of the driveway and pulled away from her house.

XX

In a decision devised to conserve strength until the last possible moment, Neil resumed partial control for the trip to the university. I suspected where Sean would be, and Neil knew exactly how to get us there.

Katherine parked her car in the Northern Oval of the University of Oklahoma. The Old Science Hall was not far from the Oval, and Neil again found himself in debate with his friends.

"Damn it, Neil," Katherine pronounced, "you are completely disoriented right now. If we weren't going to allow *Alistaire* to do this alone, what in the world makes you think we're going to abandon *you*?"

Neil shook his head, a motion which sent his mind swimming. He understood even less than they did about what was happening to him at this point, but he knew he cared about them and wanted to protect them from harm at all cost. "Kathy, I don't have any idea what to expect. All I know is that Alistaire wants into that building. How can I expect you to walk headlong into who-knows-what when even I—"

"Neil," Michael said, "shut up. We're coming with you."

Neil continued to protest even as they pulled him from the car.

The campus was auspiciously deserted, even for a summer evening. Between arguments, Neil and Mike determined that the main doors would certainly be locked by this time, and that the best way to gain entrance was through the lower floor windows, which apparently were never properly secured.

"I've partied in there after-hours more than once," Neil confessed. "The one in the middle is pretty well blocked from view by the bushes. It leads into one of the downstairs lecture rooms. We would drink or play 'Murder' or whatever. The place is pretty old and creepy and ..."

His voice trailed off. His memories had provided me with the information I needed. I reasserted myself and resumed control.

"Alistaire?" Katherine questioned.

"Yes," I told her. *"I have returned. Please be silent for a moment."* I reached out to the surrounding area. Nothing seemed terribly out of place, or perilous, at this point. Rather than engage in further debate over their presence, which would only serve to take up more time, I motioned for them to follow me.

As Neil had indicated, the middle window on the southern side of the building made for easy, secluded entrance. The lights within the building were out, but there was enough ambient glow from the outside campus lights shining through the numerous windows for even my mortal companions to see.

"This way." I led them up to the main level. The old studio theatre was locked with a chain.

"Now what?" Michael whispered.

I examined the chain, searching for the weakest link. Finding it, I grasped the links on either side of it, pulling firmly in one direction, then snapped sharply to the other. The rickety link parted just enough for me to unhook it from the rest. I then adjusted the remaining links so that the door would appear to still be locked once we were inside.

My companions in tow, I strode into the darkened house. It was now much too dark for any but myself to see, so I reluctantly turned on the house lights. I remembered the theatre now from Neil's many hours here. I hadn't recalled it being quite so confined, but that hardly mattered now. As the lights went on, I heard shuffling from the wings of the stage. I motioned for Katherine and Michael to get behind me as I called out, *"I know you are there. Show yourself."*

The shuffling froze in place, then the wing curtains parted, and Mark Hudson stepped into view.

"Alistaire?" he called out in Sean's Irish dialect, his eyes squinted against the sudden illumination. His overall appearance was quite haggard, but he otherwise seemed to have provided for himself well enough.

Perhaps too well.

"Yes, Sean," I answered, *"it's me. Step out into the light so that we can see you better."*

He did, his hand shading his eyes. "Only happy to oblige, my friend. Now why don't ye come closer so that I can see you, too."

I held my ground, studying him with my senses. As I did, my confidence in him began to grow. Karl Schaumburg's corpse had been a fairly recent kill. For Sean to have done that, then gotten back down to his hiding place to settle in before we arrived, I doubted that he would have had the chance to clean himself.

"Who is that with ye, Alistaire?" Sean asked, trying to better see my young friends. "That's not Alicia or Lora, is it?"

"No," I told him. *"These are my latest companions through Neil. They are assisting me through my time of disorientation. How have you been on your own, Sean?"*

"As well as can be expected," he said. "Mark's personality threw me off balance for a while longer than I first anticipated, but I've got things under control now."

"Do you?"

Sean frowned. "What's that supposed to mean, Alistaire?"

I finally moved down the side aisle toward him, motioning quietly for Katherine and Michael to remain where they were. *"There's been trouble, my friend. Do you recall the group of hooligans Mark and Neil skirmished with before parting ways?"*

"Aye. How could I not?"

"The two leaders are dead. So are three other people who recently caused trouble for Neil." I heard Katherine shudder, but I had to count on Michael to support her for the time being. *"I am not responsible, although the authorities are likely to suspect Neil after this latest episode."*

"And ye think that *I* did these things?" He sounded deeply, sincerely hurt.

"I do not wish to believe so, but if you didn't, then someone wanted me to think that you did."

"How so?"

"The latest victim was slain in a fashion very similar to the way I have witnessed you dispatch our enemies during our battles."

"Alistaire, believe me. I did *not* do it."

I had finally come to stand before the stage, bringing us within ten feet of each other. I could see him, smell him, feel him. He was telling the truth.

"I believe you," I told him. *"But if it was not you, and not I, then* who?*"*

Sean opened his mouth to speak, but the answering voice came from behind and above me.

"Oh, come now, Bachman, haven't you figured that out

yet?"

I spun on my heel. Leering out of the studio's control booth — a position that froze my heart as it was right behind Katherine and Michael — loomed the unexpected, blood-covered figure of Neil's friend, Alex Monroe.

Or at least, it bore the *appearance* of Alex Monroe — the voice had already told me who it really was.

"Bishop."

XXI

My flash of stunned recognition cost me dearly. Before I could act, Bishop leaped from the top of the short ladder, landing between the seats a single row behind Katherine and Michael. His hands snaked out and locked around each of their necks. They cringed and tried to pull away, but Bishop's spirit provided Alex Monroe's body with too much brawn for them to do so.

"It's been a long time, kraut," Bishop sneered.

I did not move a muscle, and, thankfully, neither did Sean. As I spoke, I measured every aspect of the situation, seeking some avenue to freeing my friends from the clutches of this British megalomaniac. *"Where did you come from, Bishop? How did you get here?"*

Bishop snickered. He slowly dragged his captives toward the center of the theatre, away from the aisles — if I wanted to reach him, I would have to go over rows of seats to do it. *"Let's see ... first, you* assumed *that you destroyed me that night in Sir Lloyd's manor. It never occurred to your pathetic, arrogant, dogmatic mind that I could escape the flames as well as you. Oh, it took me a long time to heal, and even longer for the scars to fade, but as I am intelligent enough to harbor minions, I was well provided for. Second, as to how I came to be* here, *in this world and in this body, neither you nor Carpenter ever thought about that book of self-hypnosis that Monroe borrowed but never returned, did you? Remember? He wanted more hypnotic knowledge in case there was trouble and Carpenter was 'not around?' He was quite curious. He didn't want to try on the persona of that drooling idiot zombie of yours, so he decided to tap a character of more luster. After that, it was only a matter of time."*

"I see," I nodded. Katherine and Michael stood very still as Bishop told his story. I cursed myself for allowing them to fall into such peril. How had Bishop slipped through my senses? Then again, I had once done much the same to him and his British partners. Another thing to consider: While I was still the elder, the age ratio between us had shortened considerably. Bishop was no longer a surprisingly collected *young* vampire — he had firmly come of age. I had to play this hand very carefully if I hoped to keep Michael and Katherine free from harm. No matter what deals Bishop would propose to make — and I was sure that he would do so or he would have already slain them — I knew that he ultimately intended to avenge himself upon me. And since I had once taken two close friends from him ...

"You mention Trey. Does that mean that you are familiar with the Triumvirate?"

"Oh, yes. I've watched you, Bachman. I've watched you over the years while my hate has made me strong, waiting for the perfect moment to strike you down. I could have destroyed you many times in the past centuries, as you were weakened by one confrontation or another. But I wanted to hurt *you as well as kill you. It pleased me to no end when you shacked up with your werebeast friend there ..."* Sean growled deep in his throat at that. *"... and when you took in your nigger dupe, I knew my chance would soon come. Little did I suspect that I would shortly find myself drawn into a strange, new world, a place that knows*

nothing of vampires or the supernatural but what their lore tells them. From Alex Monroe, I was able to draw even more information about you than I had before." He chuckled wickedly. "*It's too bad you and the mick know each other so well. I was really hoping you would turn on one another as you tried to do to Sir Kenton and myself. But ...*" He shook Katherine and Michael roughly. "*... I suppose things have turned out just as well. Now,*" the smile abruptly dropped from his face, and searing animosity lit his eyes, "*listen to me very carefully, kraut. If you try anything, I will tear the spines right out of your friends here before you can touch me. You and your mick friend step towar—*"

I do not know what signal they might have been waiting for, or how they could have formulated any plan under the circumstances, but as Bishop made to move further toward the right side of the theatre house, Katherine and Michael both twisted within his grasp and struck at him with all of their mortal strength. Michael landed a double-fisted blow to his midsection, and Katherine lashed her fingernails across his cheek and into his eye. Bishop bellowed in rage. Their attack did not free them, but served only to enrage him ...

... and distract him.

Sean and I moved as one. Catapulting over the chairs, we shortened the distance between us and our adversary in a heartbeat. I swept by, freeing Katherine and carrying her out of the madman's reach. Sean did the same with Michael.

"*No!*" Bishop screamed.

I shoved Katherine away as softly as I could afford, then leaped back against the British vampire. We tumbled over the seats, striking the floor and wrestling in the tight space.

"Move! Get out of here!" I heard Sean commanding. Bishop heard him as well, and he redoubled his efforts against me.

A well-placed kick shoved me away from him. He untangled himself from the chair bottoms and turned toward the theatre exit, toward the retreating figures of Katherine and Michael.

Sean slammed into him, but Bishop managed to hold his footing.

"Get away from me, werebeast!" he roared, pushing Sean away with strength that belied the size of their mortal forms. He moved after my friends, a snarl escaping his throat.

"BISHOP!" I howled at the top of my lungs.

He glanced back over his shoulder. I also had the attention of Katherine and Michael even as they reached the theatre doors. What happened next brought a gasp from Katherine, and an expression of pure shock from Michael.

My body, *Neil's* body, dissolved into my mist-like metaform. I blew across the theatre, enveloping Bishop like a shroud.

Bishop struggled within my vaporous hold, his eyes gleaming crimson, his savage, over-sized canines lashing about, trying to find something solid enough to bite.

"Jesus Christ," Michael whispered.

"Oh, God, oh, God, oh, God ..." Katherine murmured over and over again. They had frozen in their tracks. Sean hurried to them, and I could see through my hazy vision that he was in quarter-wolf form. He said something to them, probably telling them to leave, but I believe it was his inhuman appearance, not his words, that made them comply.

Twisting about, Bishop shifted into his bat guise, a form covered with the animal hair that had led me to suspect Sean of Karl Schaumburg's murder, and finally slithered out of my nebulous grasp.

"Ye're going nowhere, vampire!" Sean barreled into the British immortal, the Irishman's body now past the half-wolf mark. I solidified to assist him, and I am certain my eyes glowed white within Neil Carpenter's face.

The man-bat slashed and struck the man-wolf, and Sean staggered before the strength of the undead. Bishop made to strike at him further before I again fell upon him.

"Leave, Sean!" I yelled to my partner. *"This is personal business to which I must attend."*

"But, Alistaire—"

"Go!" I commanded as Bishop almost slipped away. He bit down on my hand, and I recoiled with the pain. *"Protect Katherine and Michael! Now!"*

Sean growled his disapproval, then left.

"Now, my British nemesis," I snarled, *"it is just you and me."*

"Excellent!" he agreed with a twisted grin. *"No werewolf to help you!"*

"And no Brigade to help you."

But his vicious smile only broadened. *"Indeed."* He absently ran a finger through the still-damp gore soaked into his shirt, then licked it away. *"I have fed well this evening. Tell me, kraut, have* you?*"*

The battle that ensued belittled even my age-old confrontation with Sir Kenton. The shades of our mortal forms no longer colored our abilities, and we struck and bit and lashed at each other with our full vampiric powers. I *had* wondered about Bishop's fate from time to time — after all, I had never actually *seen* his burning corpse. Now was my chance to close a chapter on my past.

My moment of reflection cost me dearly. Bishop dove forward and bit into the side of my neck.

I staggered backward, tripping over something loose on the floor and falling flat on my back. I raised my arms, expecting Bishop to descend upon me like a vulture.

He did not. He was out of the theatre before I realized

he was going after Sean and Michael ...

... and Katherine.

Fear gripped my heart as I dissolved into mist and pursued him. Out through the lobby, down the stairwell, and through the basement hallway I soared.

I found them in the lecture room through which we had entered the building. Michael was shoving Katherine through the window, and Sean, now in complete wolfen form, snarled and bit at Bishop to keep him away, heedless of the damage the British vampire was causing to him in return.

I sailed through the air, returning to humanoid form at the top of my arc, and alighted upon Bishop's back. We collapsed to the floor together and resumed our struggle. Bishop rolled and coiled and ended up on top of me. He landed several thundering blows across my face, and I struggled to remain lucid.

"This is your end, kraut!" he hissed, lashing his talons across my chest. *"I'm going to destroy you, then your mick servant, and then your new little friends."* He leaned in closer, his claws digging into my neck, his teeth gleaming, his eyes glowing. *"And then, who knows? Maybe the rest of those children you've befriended. And then Carpenter's whole family, and then ... "*

"ENOUGH!"

But my cry was grandiose. My attempt to roll away from him failed, and Bishop laughed as he landed yet another blow across my face. My vision began to dim.

A blur of movement marked Sean's passage as he slammed into Bishop, at last knocking him off of me.

"I have had enough of you*!"* Bishop roared at the enormous wolf. He feigned with a clawed hand, then kicked when Sean made to evade. A loud crunch echoed through the darkened lecture room as the wolf's foreleg broke, and

Sean yelped in pain.

I tried to shift again into mist form but found my concentration was insufficient, so I leaped upon Bishop once more.

"That is the last time *you will harm anyone, ever again,"* I promised.

Bishop hissed a vicious laugh, and knocked me aside. He pinned me to the floor, laughed again, and leaned over my neck, his jaws open wide. Sean limped into the scene, but another kick from Bishop sent him reeling.

"I have waited a long time for this, kraut," he told me. *"My hate is stronger than your faith."*

I felt his breath on my face, and his teeth brushed against the flesh of my throat.

A chair crashed against Bishop's back, splintering harmlessly but jarring him just enough for me to free a single hand. I reached forward and dug my fingertips deep into his chest. He winced in pain and tried to draw back, but I pulled up my legs and locked them around the small of his back. He was going nowhere.

I informed him, *"This is your end."*

My fingers pressed deeper, breaking through flesh and muscle and bone. Bishop fought to free himself, then changed tactics and stretched out.

Katherine, who still stood over us holding the remains of the chair she had used against Bishop, shrieked when Bishop's hand latched onto her leg. She fell and struggled desperately to crawl away from him, but his hold was too strong.

"If this is my *end,"* Bishop said to me through clenched teeth, *"then it is* hers *as well."* He pulled her in.

Then Michael and Sean were there. Sean reverted to half-wolf form, and they anchored Katherine. Her leg bled as her flesh tore from the force of the struggle, but Bishop could drag her no closer.

"I think not," I said, and my hand broke way into his chest. Bishop cried out, and cursed me one last time as I wrenched and extracted his heart.

"Damn you to hell, *Bachman,"* he said, and collapsed.

Then we all lay there, and thanked *God*.

POSTSCRIPT

Michael's family had long retired by the time we reached his house. Sean, Katherine, and I treated our wounds as quietly and cleanly as possible. When morning grew near, I knew I would soon have to relinquish control to Neil for one of the last times. I thanked Michael deeply, and we departed. He will claim that he parted ways with Neil and Katherine earlier in the evening, and knows nothing of what happened at the university. With the apparent body of Alex Monroe added to the list of bloodshed, Neil Carpenter and Mark Hudson have little time left.

Katherine tried to convince me to let her join us, but I would have nothing of it. I reminded her that her brother still needs her — *everyone* will need her open mind as the supernatural continues to pervade your world. She fought bravely against her tears as we left her near her house — I suspect that, given the nature of her father's death, and the condition in which her brother was no doubt found, the authorities will not be too skeptical when she feigns a similarly distraught and *amnesiac* state of mind.

Sean and I have little in the way of finances, but with centuries of experience behind me, I shall find a way to put us on our feet soon enough. We shall relocate to a larger city to begin our new crusade ... perhaps Pittsburgh, perhaps not.

In one final plea, Neil begged for a chance to bid

farewell to his loved ones. I was reluctant at first until he suggested that one way to accomplish this was to write this very narration. Who knows? When more and more corpses are found with twin holes in the throat and no blood in the body, when more wild animals are hunted, only to leave a human carcass when finally brought down, when the dead begin to refuse to stay dead, perhaps someone out there will read this, and begin to wonder.

As you may have surmised, Neil Carpenter is now gone. I regret that this was necessary. I may be a vampire, but I believe I have clearly indicated my abhorrence to the taking of innocent life. Still, I will be needed here, and if I have sacrificed dozens of lifetimes to God's work, is it really so much to ask that Neil sacrifice part of just one? Perhaps this sounds cold, but there are difficult times ahead, and I can delay no longer. Tomorrow night I will leave this manuscript at Neil's home, then we leave.

Who knows how long it will take us to get where we are going? After all, we have to keep our eyes open for Trey Matthews along the way.

Geh mit Gott,
Go with God,
Alistaire Bachman.

BE SURE TO WATCH FOR

CONNEXION

THE SHORT-STORY SEQUEL TO
PANDORA'S GAME

SOON TO BE RELEASED IN THE
COLLECTED WORKS
THE DARKNESS WITHIN

AND DON'T MISS
THE NEXT TRIUMVIRATE NOVEL

OF WOLF AND MAN

ABOUT THE AUTHOR

CHRISTOPHER ANDREWS has been writing since the age of seven. While attending University of Oklahoma, he completed two novels, *Refuge Among the Stars* (1989) and *The Blue Man* (1991), and a series of short-stories. In 1992, he co-created and wrote the premier issue of the comic book *The Triumvirate*, and sold his first screenplay, "Thirst," to RF Video Productions.

In May of 1992, Christopher received a Bachelor's Degree in Theatre, and that August he traveled to California to pursue a career in acting — and he continued to write. In 1994, he co-plotted and scripted the premier of Derek Lipscomb's comic book, *The Golden Scarab*, for Sharp Eye Graphix. In 1995, he co-wrote the science-fiction screenplay, *Dream Parlor*, with Jonathan Lawrence.

In 1999, he completed and published his third novel, *Pandora's Game*. And the *Dream Parlor* movie — in which he starred — premiered.

Over the next few years, Christopher completed and published three more novels: *Dream Parlor* (2000), the novelization of the film; *Paranormals* (2002); and *Hamlet: Prince of Denmark* (2005), the novelization of Shakespeare's play. And his short-stories "Mistake" and "Thirst" were adapted into short-films in 2004 and 2005, respectively.

Today, Christopher lives in California with his wife, Yvonne Isaak-Andrews. He is working on his seventh novel, *Of Wolf and Man*, the long-awaited sequel to *Pandora's Game*, and continues to work as an actor — *Dream Parlor* the movie is now available on DVD, and his next feature-film starring role, *Drivetime of the Dead*, is in post-production.

Excerpts from all of Christopher's novels can be found at www.dreamparlor.com.

Printed in the United States
60970LVS00005B/2